T0281975

DEVIOUS WEB

DEVIOUS WEB

A NOVEL

SHELLEY GRANDY

Published by SparkPress, a BookSparks imprint,
A division of SparkPoint Studio, LLC
Phoenix, Arizona, USA, 85007
www.gosparkpress.com

Published 2024
Printed in the United States of America
Print ISBN: 978-1-68463-274-9
E-ISBN: 978-1-68463-275-6
Library of Congress Control Number: 2024911369

Interior design by Tabitha Lahr

To my husband Roy, daughter Erin,
and granddaughters Emilia and Olivia.

PELLUCID:

1: admitting maximum passage of light without diffusion or distortion: *a pellucid stream*
2: reflecting light evenly from all surfaces
3: easy to understand.

— *Merriam-Webster*

PART ONE

 *Chapter 1:*

TOM AND LAWRENCE—JULY 29, 2021

The pandemic had not been kind to Lawrence Cameron, at least not to his waistline. As The Big Guy strode across the restaurant to join him for dinner, Tom could easily see that Lawrence had packed on a few more pounds while working from home. Toronto's legendary finance guru and media commentator had earned his nickname for his investing prowess, but now the term was even more suitable for the six-foot-two-inch, 250-pound influencer.

When Tom stood to greet him at their table, Lawrence gave him his usual whack on the back and the now customary COVID-19 elbow bump. Even though Tom had played football in high school and was himself six feet tall, he always felt dwarfed by his main investor and personal mentor. Maybe it was also because of the gap in experience between them, as Lawrence was twenty years older.

"Tom, how's my favorite entrepreneur doing?" Lawrence asked while settling into the comfortable leather banquette reserved especially for him by the manager of ONE, the see-and-be-seen restaurant adjacent to the Hazelton Hotel in Toronto's upscale Yorkville enclave.

"Good, thanks, Lawrence, but crazy busy with all that's going on with the business, as you can imagine," Tom responded.

"No doubt. And I bet you never thought that seven years in, you would have brought Pellucid so far!" Lawrence said.

Tom agreed as he reflected on how truly surreal it was that the data analytics software company he had founded—Pellucid—was valued at over US $200 million, and a Silicon Valley company was now proposing an acquisition.

To have hit that milestone at the age of thirty-eight is honestly mind-blowing, Tom thought.

"I'm looking forward to hearing your updates today, Tom, but given that Grace just put me on a no-frills diet, I'm definitely ready to dive into this menu before we get started," Lawrence joked.

Tom smiled, knowing that Lawrence's second wife, Grace, did her best to keep her husband's life—and his weight—balanced. He knew Lawrence would be eyeing the restaurant's signature lobster spoons as an appetizer and something carb-heavy and definitely not on Grace's diet plan for the main course.

While Lawrence ordered for them, Tom admired the contemporary styling of the chic restaurant.

It's the little things everyone missed during the restrictions of the pandemic, like being able to get together with friends or enjoying this kind of ambience, Tom thought.

Yorkville, with its high-end boutiques and elegant hotels and restaurants, was where Toronto's elite dined and shopped. It wasn't part of Tom's typical day-to-day, but he and his wife, Miriam, sometimes had drinks at ONE's expansive bar because the art gallery she curated was just around the corner.

After the waiter had filled their glasses with a Chianti Classico wine, Lawrence leaned forward and spoke quietly so other diners wouldn't overhear.

"So, what about the acquisition? What's the latest from Crystal Clere?" he asked.

Tom confided that the California artificial intelligence company's CEO had confirmed he would be offering US $250 million in cash and stock to acquire Pellucid. The next step would be for Tom to receive a letter of intent formalizing the offer, and then Pellucid's board would have until September 15—about six weeks—to decide whether to approve the sale.

"I'm open to the offer, which is certainly substantial, but I still feel a bit reluctant, Lawrence. I always envisioned taking Pellucid to an IPO on the TSX and Nasdaq myself. On the other hand, it's hard to turn down a huge payout from a well-established company like Crystal Clere that's a great fit for our software," Tom said.

"Not only that, Tom, but as they say, timing is everything. The pandemic has shown you never know what kind of economic climate you might encounter just when you're ready to take the company public. Sometimes it's good to take a profit and focus on the next opportunity," Lawrence said, as he nodded to acknowledge a couple of people passing by their table who obviously recognized the Big Guy from media interviews.

"That's a great point, especially after everything we've seen over the last year, from market volatility to the January 6 insurrection," Tom agreed. "It definitely creates a more opportunistic mindset."

"And of course, I wouldn't object if my investment in Pellucid netted out to a nice-sized return," Lawrence quipped.

"Ha, I'm sure!" Tom replied. "Well, for now, Winston is earning his CFO pay and then some, working through the due diligence to address all the financials, and Crystal Clere's CEO and I are in discussions ensuring we're well aligned. But so far, I can say that I like what I see. And that's important because if we sell, they'll probably want me and possibly a couple of my senior team to commit to working for a year or so as part of Crystal Clere."

"Yes, it's pretty standard for the acquiring company to want at least the CEO to stay on for continuity," Lawrence agreed. "Overall, you've got this, Tom. Working through the process, making sure you have all the information up front, and doing the due diligence is the right approach. Then when you have all the facts and feel comfortable, I'm sure it will be easier to make your final decision. And, of course, whatever direction you decide to take, the board of directors must be onside with it as well."

Tom nodded agreement as Lawrence twirled some of his impressively presented main-course seafood linguini onto his fork.

"Okay, so fill me in on Patrick," Lawrence said. "I know you were having some issues with him last time we talked. How did that net out?"

Tom sighed. It had been a tough situation to manage. Five years before, Tom had met Patrick McGowan at the stable where they both boarded horses and had soon hired Patrick to be his business development manager. The two men were close in age but had vastly different personalities. While Patrick's Irish flair and direct manner with prospects had proven helpful in building the business, his proclivity for partying had created problems.

Tom shared with Lawrence that he'd had no choice but to fire Patrick and, after a contentious final meeting with him, he suspected their friendship had been permanently shattered.

"That's unfortunate, Tom," Lawrence said. "But eventually Patrick's shenanigans would have attracted attention and reflected badly on Pellucid. I know you hate being tough on people, but didn't he lose an investor for you when he missed a key meeting?"

Tom indicated that had indeed been the last straw and agreed he had run out of options when it came to keeping Patrick on his payroll.

The two men lingered over coffee and liqueurs while reviewing Pellucid's latest quarterly results, upcoming sales pipeline, and the company's case study currently in development at Tom's father-in-law's business in North Carolina, one of Tom's biggest early-stage clients.

"Are you staying here in Yorkville tonight or at your place?" Tom asked as he and Lawrence concluded their business.

"Next door at the Hazelton," Lawrence replied. "Grace and I have been living up north at the cottage during the pandemic, and I'm more comfortable playing tourist here in Yorkville rather than rattling around our big house in Rosedale without Grace."

Tom chuckled at Lawrence's candor and, as always, admired the close relationship Lawrence had with his wife. The two men parted ways, with Lawrence going to the bar for a final nightcap before turning in and Tom heading for home.

 Chapter 2:

TOM—JULY 29

The sun was setting when Tom left the restaurant, and as the warm July air enveloped him, he felt that everything—or at least almost everything—was falling into place.

Having Lawrence as a sounding board was always helpful when navigating tough decisions as CEO. But Tom knew that, along with resolving the acquisition issue, he needed to address some gaps in his personal life.

He had been consumed with work and putting aside concerns about his relationship with Miriam. His marriage was the one puzzle piece out of place and, as he stepped out onto the sidewalk on Yorkville Avenue to find his Uber, Tom promised himself he would face up to that.

Just then there was a sudden screech of tires as a black SUV launched itself over the curb, aiming straight for him. Tom was barely able to dodge aside before the vehicle veered back onto the road and sped away.

As he leaned against the restaurant's exterior wall and caught his breath, Tom felt shaken after such a close call—and he doubted it was accidental.

Chapter 3:

ELISE AND WINSTON—JULY 29

T he Pellucid office, located in a typical older downtown building in Toronto's Entertainment District, combined historical charm—brick walls and soaring leaded windows—with modern decor and the latest in electronic equipment, including smart lighting and Sonos wireless speakers in every room. There was also a fully equipped kitchen and a large lounge area that made the space a good home away from home for the team who had spent many hours working there, as is common at early-stage companies.

However, the office had been closed since the start of the pandemic and only recently reopened with limited attendance to enable social distancing. It was almost a luxury for employees to come back after the confinement of working from home in small condos or townhouses. Although quite a few Pellucid employees were sick with COVID, fortunately none had to be hospitalized.

Elise Armstrong, Pellucid's chief marketing officer, was glad to be able to reconnect with staff today in person and welcomed things getting back to a semblance of normal. But when she walked into the office bathroom, she had to admit that seeing herself in the mirror under the glare of harsh office lighting was a bit of a shock. She looked so pale it was obvious she had been working too many hours and getting little sun this summer. She would pick up some bronzer as soon as possible and try to look more alive.

And she was also going to get out of shape fast if she didn't make a point of getting to the stable to ride. She was part-boarding a horse at the barn where Tom and Patrick kept their horses in Caledon, about an hour northwest of downtown Toronto, but her visits to the stable had been less frequent lately due to COVID restrictions and because of work. Elise's mom had assured her that she was highly unlikely to gain weight on her five-foot-nine-inch frame, but her mother was no doubt biased.

While she touched up her lip gloss, Elise couldn't help thinking that men were lucky they didn't have to concern themselves as much with appearances. But in her role, she was often on Zoom calls, speaking at events, or meeting with journalists, so she needed to present herself well. And Elise's thirty-third birthday was coming up soon, so she scrutinized her reflection in the mirror, looking for the first sign of gray.

None so far, thankfully, Elise noted, as she smoothed her long blond hair and went out to the office's lounge area for a bite to eat with Winston Wilson, Pellucid's chief financial officer. The Uber Eats delivery person arrived with their sandwiches and salads, and she poked her head into Winston's office to let him know the food had arrived. Elise picked up a half sandwich and sank into a cushy armchair.

Winston had seemed preoccupied lately, and Elise suspected it was more than just the acquisition that was consuming his attention. A handsome Black man in his early forties with solid business experience acquired working for tech companies in Chicago and Toronto, he had always been something of an enigma. Tom had commented to her that Winston reminded him of a high-stakes poker player whose expression rarely offered a clue to what he was thinking.

So it was no surprise that Winston shared very little of his private life except for his fondness for a couple of nieces back home in Atlanta, Georgia, to whom, Elise gathered, he sent money from time to time. If it was a personal issue bothering Winston, he undoubtedly wouldn't share it with her.

Elise could relate to Winston's reserve because she had a secret of her own that she had only recently admitted to herself. She had done some soul-searching when her mother asked why she wasn't dating, something Elise had attributed to being busy with her career. But when she was honest with herself, Elise realized that no one measured up to Tom in her eyes. She was totally captivated by her boss, Tom Oliver, and her feelings were only growing stronger.

In addition to the fact that his tall, athletic build and intense blue eyes made him her exact type, Elise loved that Tom was quietly unassuming despite being an impressive guy. He had a sharp, insightful mind and great entrepreneurial instincts, but he also had a high EQ and was always down-to-earth with people. The Pellucid team knew Tom had their back. And for Elise, being with Tom felt like a perfect fit.

Elise hoped she had successfully managed to hide her feelings—because Tom had been married to Miriam for quite some time before she had met him. Elise had wondered lately if all was well with Tom and Miriam, but she would never do anything to interfere with their relationship. She had accepted that she would have to be satisfied with spending time with Tom at the office and riding together when they had the chance.

"Elise, is everything okay?" Winston asked her as she held the half sandwich in her hand, staring out the window.

Elise smiled and said, "Yes, just thinking about my rather long to-do list, which is distracting when I'm supposed to be eating."

"You deserve a break," Winston said kindly while grabbing a plate and loading up on food. "You've been doing an awesome job getting us media coverage. And there's been lots of positive feedback ever since the *Financial Post* magazine profiled Tom in their 2020 Top Forty Under Forty feature."

"Thanks, Winston. Hopefully it all adds up to Crystal Clere seeing us as a hot commodity," Elise noted.

Winston agreed, and Elise was pleased to see his shoulders relax a little as he apologetically excused himself, taking the rest of his dinner to his desk to start another night of number-crunching.

Elise wondered what he was brooding over aside from the acquisition. She was convinced there was more and wished she could help. But for now, it was back to work for her too, prepping Tom's talking points for a *Bloomberg News* interview the next day.

 *Chapter 4:*

TOM AND DETECTIVE LIU—JULY 30

Detective Jason Liu was in his office at the Toronto Police Service's downtown College Street headquarters having his second coffee of the day and reviewing case files when the front desk let him know that a Tom Oliver was asking to see him. Liu was surprised but said to send Tom up to his seventh-floor office.

"Tom! What brings you here?" Liu said as he got up to greet his old friend.

"Well, first let me apologize for not having gotten together for a while," Tom said.

"No worries. I think all of us have had fewer get-togethers during the pandemic. I've seen you pop up in the finance news, and it looks like Pellucid is going strong," Liu responded.

"Yes, I can't complain about that. But I'm here on something a bit more up your alley," Tom said. "A bizarre incident happened last night, and I'd like your opinion if you have time?"

"Of course," Liu said, intrigued, as he gestured for Tom to take a seat in the only available chair. Heaps of paperwork and file folders occupied the other two office chairs, which worked well as a deterrent to any time-wasting colleagues who might distract from Liu's day.

Tom explained to Liu that he had almost been struck by a black BMW SUV when he came out of ONE restaurant in Yorkville the previous night. Had he not moved aside quickly and if the car hadn't swerved back onto the road, it could have ended terribly.

"Did you get a look at the driver, or did anyone get the license plate number?" Liu asked.

"No, it all happened too fast," Tom said.

"Was there any reason for the vehicle to veer onto the sidewalk?

"Nothing—perfect driving conditions with little traffic," Tom said.

"And I'm assuming the driver just kept going—didn't stop to check if you were okay?"

"Yes, they just took off," Tom confirmed.

The detective frowned.

"Jason, I wouldn't expect you to be able to do anything about a random situation like that with absolutely nothing to go on other than the make of car," Tom continued. "But I thought I'd run it by you because I've also had the uneasy feeling lately that I'm being followed. It's happened a few times downtown when I've left the office. Obviously, it makes me wonder how random that was last night."

Liu raised his eyebrows when he heard Tom's story and said understatedly, "That's not good."

Liu and his parents had moved to Toronto from Hong Kong when he was starting high school, and he and Tom were in the same class and had been friends ever since—more like brothers really—so Liu had no intention of brushing off this situation.

"Tom, do you have any reason to suspect someone of having it in for you? Any enemies or issues you can think of at all?" Liu continued.

Tom looked thoughtful for a moment and shrugged. "I've been asking myself that, and I'm coming up blank. I mean somewhere along the way someone could have felt resentful about not being hired for a job or losing out on a competitive bid. But no, I can't think of any enemies," Tom said.

"Any recent firings or issues at the office?" Liu asked.

"Yes, I had to fire my business development manager, Patrick McGowan, who was also a friend, but it wouldn't even cross my mind that Patrick would do something like that," Tom said.

"How did he take the news of being let go?"

"Not very graciously. He was resentful and pretty vocal about it, but I already knew he has a hot temper," Tom conceded.

"Hmm." Liu made a couple of notes and tapped his pen on the desk, as he tended to do when thinking things through.

"So, what if it's less about you personally and more about the company? Is there any controversy happening behind the scenes?" Liu asked.

Tom explained confidentially about the possible acquisition and the sizable amount of money involved. He added that the Pellucid board of directors was divided in terms of whether to accept the offer, but there was no apparent animosity about the situation which would be resolved by mid-September one way or the other.

"What about specific competitors? Does anyone have an axe to grind?" Liu asked.

Tom outlined that at least two other companies, one in Canada and the other in the United States, offered similar software platforms that weren't as mature as Pellucid's, but neither company had ever made any trouble for him.

Liu made more notes and put his pen down.

"Well, here's my take on this. If someone is following you, and you're being targeted, it could be someone you know or someone who was impacted by Pellucid. Or it could be some random person who has seen you in the media and resents your success. There's no way to know unless someone tips their hand," Liu said.

"A random stalker seems a bit of a stretch, don't you think?" Tom commented.

"In my world of homicide investigations, anything is possible. Fact is, you're CEO of a company that's being offered multimillions at a time when numerous businesses have closed during the pandemic, lots of people have lost their jobs, and many are struggling with their mental health. Of course, no one outside your inner circle knows that you have a pending acquisition offer, but it's obvious from the positive media coverage you're getting that Pellucid is doing well. So, someone could be jealous or resentful and taking it out on you as the poster boy for entrepreneurs," Liu said.

"Ha, hardly," Tom responded.

"Seriously, Tom, no matter who is involved, you need to be careful. Continue listening to your intuition, be aware of your surroundings all the time, and call me any time of day or night if you have any concerns whatsoever. Don't be a hero just because you were the high school quarterback," Liu teased.

Tom smiled and nodded, and Liu hoped he would take his advice to heart. Liu added that he would check with the restaurant and neighboring businesses for any security footage in case that could shed some light on who had been behind the wheel. He would also create a general occurrence report so the incident would be on file in case of any future issues.

Then, because it was the polite thing to do, Liu asked after Miriam, and Tom said she was doing well.

Liu had never been a fan of Miriam and couldn't see the attraction. That relationship was a fait accompli by the time Liu met her. Tom and Miriam had connected in London, England while Tom was doing his master's and she had traveled there from her home in North Carolina for an art history course.

Liu attributed the fast engagement and the affinity between Tom and Miriam to the fact that Tom's parents had been killed in a car accident at the end of his final undergrad year, and Miriam's mother had died of pancreatic cancer at about the same time. *Maybe being able to relate to each other's losses had masked the major differences in their backgrounds and personalities,* Liu thought.

"And how is your brother, Nate? I haven't seen his name cross my desk, so that's a good thing," Liu said.

"Unfortunately, Nate is the same, Jason. Still an alcoholic but at least keeping a job these days. I only see him when he comes in to hit me up for cash or to pay off a credit card over-run. It's hard to believe he got the same inheritance I did from our parents' estate," Tom said. "It's disappointing that he has such an entitled attitude—like I owe him something—instead of treating me like a brother."

"I'm sorry to hear that. I know you try hard with him, but it's always been a one-way street," Liu said. "Maybe Nate staying out of trouble is the best we can hope for."

Tom nodded in agreement and asked about Liu's parents, who had always been very kind to him, and then said he would let Liu get on with his day. Liu suggested that they meet for a drink sometime on a patio when things at work calmed down for Tom, whenever that might be.

 *Chapter 5:*

PATRICK—AUGUST 3

Patrick was at his Leslieville duplex taking a break from searching job sites on his iPhone, instead scanning through his recent photos. He paused on one from his recent trip to Las Vegas.

That was the debacle that had finished things at Pellucid, Patrick thought, looking at the happy faces in the photo. *But what a blast it was!*

It was among the first big tech trade shows slated since the pandemic hit, and everyone was in a celebratory mood, especially himself, Patrick recalled. Tom had asked him to attend ISC West, an international security conference staged in mid-July. Tom was always thinking of new ventures, and he was considering plans to further develop Pellucid's data analytics as a tool for security software.

Patrick was to scope out the latest internet of things (IoT) security innovations and meet with the business development lead for an emerging IT security company. A potential investor attending the show from San Diego had also connected with Tom, so that would be an important meeting. Patrick was on deck to potentially arrange an infusion of capital for Pellucid.

He had a busy agenda for the three-day event. These things are always exhausting, with miles to walk up and down the exhibit hall checking out innovations, plus the demands of networking events and meetings. And, of course, if you're someone like him who loves Las Vegas, the nightlife deserves its share of attention.

Las Vegas was already Patrick's playground. He typically liked to get there at least four times a year to have a good time and gamble. And he gambled enough money that Vegas hotels comped his stays. It cost casino operators little for food and accommodation compared with the amount spent at the tables by high rollers.

ISE West 2021 was being held at Patrick's favorite venue, the Venetian Hotel and Expo. Patrick loved the Venetian because of its variety of restaurants with great Mediterranean fare and its fun design modeled, of course, after Venice. The hotel had an indoor canal with gondolas traveling from one end to the other and gondoliers loudly singing classic Italian songs as they floated past the restaurants and shops. Patrick had been to Venice on holiday with his parents as a teenager when he lived at home in Dublin, and he had fallen in love with the romance of the city itself.

On this trip, Patrick promised himself he would find time to book a show at the Tuscany Suites and Casino called "The Rat Pack is Back." It recreated the glory years of the original Rat Pack of Frank Sinatra, Sammy Davis Jr., Dean Martin, Joey Bishop, and Peter Lawford, and Patrick was excited to see how the imitators fared in representing the famous friends and performers. Patrick's father was a huge Frank Sinatra fan, admiring not just his singing but also his brash New York style.

Patrick's mantra for Las Vegas had long been the old "What happens in Vegas stays in Vegas." Not to brag, but women seemed to like his footballer build from playing what Americans call soccer, as well as his black hair and dark eyes. And it didn't hurt that he tended to splash out a lot of money at the gaming tables and in the bars.

While some guys traveling on business had to avail themselves of ladies for hire, Patrick usually attracted young women working at the casinos or restaurants or free-spirited women on vacation looking for a good time. A comment on his Irish accent was often the opening line for women wanting to connect with him.

In thinking back to ISE West, Patrick gave himself full marks for his first day in Vegas. He had diligently checked out possibilities for Pellucid collaborations with IoT software companies and managed to steer clear of what an old-school former boss of Patrick's used to call booth babes—women who worked hard to attract people to company booths during events but who sometimes had side jobs at night.

Patrick's meeting with the business development guy Tom had lined up went well. And he'd thoroughly enjoyed the Rat Pack retrospective show that night. He had even been lucky enough to grab a photo with the Frank Sinatra impersonator and sent it to his dad in Ireland—who had been delighted. He had kept his gambling to a reasonable limit and slept well before the trade show opened again.

It was the second day of the conference that was his undoing.

With so many stunning women everywhere you look in Vegas, a person almost gets numb to it. But when he turned a corner in the Venetian just outside the restaurant where he had gone for coffee, he saw probably the most attractive woman he had ever encountered.

She had violet eyes like iconic actress Elizabeth Taylor, with thick black flowing hair that she had deliberately highlighted with streaks of purple to complement her eyes. She wore a fitted black pantsuit with no shirt underneath, just ample cleavage discreetly displayed, and Patrick was enthralled. She fixed those spectacular violet eyes on him and smiled. Patrick approached and struck up a conversation.

This beauty, Samantha, worked with a talent agency in Las Vegas and had been hired by a Boston-based company to greet visitors and bring them into their booth to build their prospect list. Samantha also did some modeling and was part of a show playing at a downtown casino. She gave Patrick a ticket for that night and encouraged him with a wink to come to the show and join her afterward.

Patrick had an early dinner and headed to the nine o'clock show. It was something of a burlesque performance and the girls were all topless, which wasn't hard to take. With a lead role and looking amazing, Samantha was front and center—and she paid special attention to him as she performed various dance routines.

Following the show, Samantha gave Patrick a backstage tour, and it wasn't long before they were making out in the hallway. From there they moved to her dressing room, and Patrick hoisted Samantha up onto her makeup table. She had other assets in addition to her beautiful eyes, Patrick thought, as he realized it didn't matter if those amazing breasts were natural. He was surprised that the mirror attached to the makeup table survived their first encounter.

After that auspicious start, the night was filled with drinking and taking Samantha's favorite party drug, MDMA, plus more sex and gambling.

Patrick woke up the next day in his hotel room, and it was already noon. Somehow, he had miraculously made it there in one piece. There was a note beside him saying, "Thanks for the good time, sweetie," signed Samantha. Patrick's wallet was empty, so he figured they must have had a good night indeed, since US $1,500 was gone. Fortunately, his credit cards were intact.

He realized as his aching head throbbed that he had missed Tom's carefully orchestrated meeting with the investor. And the show closed in two hours. After a panicky shower and much coffee, Patrick trusted his stomach to stay in place while he called the guy's cell. No answer. Then he called the front desk. Sure enough, the prospect had been staying at the Venetian but had already checked out and was probably on a flight back to San Diego. There was no fixing this one.

Patrick was booked to return home to Toronto that night, and he wasn't looking forward to reporting the missed opportunity to Tom. At least the photos on his phone chronicled a night to remember, even if he couldn't recall all of it.

Because of the surrounding mountains, planes taking off from Vegas climb at a steep angle. As his WestJet flight took off at what felt like a vertical trajectory, Patrick suspected his career was headed in the opposite direction. And he had been right.

By the time he got back to Toronto, Tom was already livid. The investor headed a growth fund that was looking to drop $10 million into promising companies like Pellucid. But now, he was no longer interested in Pellucid since, as he said emphatically to Tom, "The company was so cavalier as to blow off meetings with no notice."

Patrick had already had an uncomfortable discussion with Tom a couple of months before when Tom addressed his behavior and how it reflected on Pellucid. Tom had made it clear that he didn't care what Patrick got up to on his own time, but it was not acceptable when it impacted the business.

It was shortly after the flight back to Toronto that he was fired, although it was discreetly positioned as "Patrick is moving on to pursue the next opportunity in his career."

It made Patrick's blood boil to think how easily he had been tossed aside, even after all the lucrative client business he had attracted to Pellucid.

He pulled up a closeup shot of beautiful Samantha on his phone. *It was all down to those eyes.*

With a sigh, he closed his photos and opened LinkedIn to resume his job search.

 *Chapter 6:*

TOM AND MIRIAM—AUGUST 14

Finally it was Saturday, and Tom was enjoying his morning coffee while gazing out at their quiet street in Toronto's Summerhill neighborhood from the vantage point of a living room wingback chair. Their house was positioned at the top of a cul-de-sac, surrounded by manicured lawns, stately trees, and elegant houses—a secure retreat that made his earlier concerns about personal safety seem unreal.

It had been two weeks since the incident in Yorkville, and Liu had let Tom know that there was no useful security footage of his near miss. Thankfully, nothing else had happened to cause concern, with no more instances of feeling he was being stalked. Tom concluded it had been a one-off situation. And he had been too busy with work to give it further thought anyway.

Tom was feeling more than ready to disengage from Pellucid for the day. He had a hard-and-fast rule that he never worked on Saturdays, with his morning always reserved to ride his horse, Titan. He would drive to the stable in Caledon as soon as he had breakfast with Miriam. And she would be off to the art gallery for her busiest day of the week.

He planned to suggest to Miriam that they have dinner at her favorite restaurant that night so they could talk on neutral territory. There were still barriers between them that needed tackling. And one of the biggest stresses on their marriage was undoubtedly her father, James P. Robinson, who lived in Raleigh, North Carolina.

Tom very much regretted that when he founded Pellucid seven years before, he had accepted seed money from James in exchange for a seat on the board of directors and shares in the company. It had been advantageous for his father-in-law's company to trial and adopt early-stage versions of Pellucid's software—and ultimately become a lead customer. But now, James was adamant that Tom should not sell Pellucid at this point and planned to vote against the acquisition when the board considered the offer at its September meeting.

It seemed ironic that Miriam, in her subdued but steely Southern style, was tenaciously supporting her father's viewpoint. Miriam was usually more concerned with keeping up with her socialite clients' lifestyles and her next home decor project than with the business. Miriam was also on Pellucid's board of directors, although more in name than function in an observer role, attending the minimum number of meetings required of her. Most days Tom steered away from talking about Pellucid at home given Miriam's total lack of interest— and her annoyance at any mention of Elise.

Tom tried to overlook his wife's tendency to support her father's opinions, since he knew she had understandably become extremely close to her dad after her mother passed away. But there were other more fundamental differences between Miriam and Tom resulting from their dissimilar upbringings—Miriam as a society girl in Raleigh and part of a stalwart conservative Republican family, and Tom the son of a liberal-leaning Canadian police officer father, who subsequently became police chief, and his mom, a public-school teacher. He was aware that James would have preferred Tom to be a conservative evangelical, joining them for Sunday services and Bible readings.

As Tom took his coffee cup to the kitchen, he was thinking that the only good thing about the pandemic was that James couldn't travel to Canada, and Tom only had to spend time with him over Zoom. Both James and his private plane had been grounded, and that worked out well.

Tom was gathering up his riding gear in the mudroom when he heard Miriam come downstairs and then call out for him to help her in the kitchen. He found her standing like a ballerina on pointe atop a step stool, trying to reach the highest kitchen cupboard.

"Miriam, you're going to kill yourself climbing up like that!" Tom exclaimed.

With his hands on her waist, Tom lifted her down, and said in mock sternness, "Don't do that again!"

"Well, maybe when you grab the omelet pan for me, you can try making something good in it," Miriam said, making a face at Tom.

At five-feet-four and with a petite build, Miriam had no hope of reaching the top shelf without a ladder. Tom was thinking that, with her dark hair pulled up into a high ponytail this morning, she looked like she could be back in university. Things seemed lighter between them, and it was a relaxed Saturday morning until her iPhone rang. James was calling, and the atmosphere changed.

"Yes, Daddy, Tom and I have been talking about it and he still feels we should keep an open mind until the something diligence is done . . . yes, the due diligence."

Miriam mouthed to Tom, "Do you want to talk to him?" and he shook his head.

"Oh, it's his riding morning and he's pretty much on his

way, so he can't talk right now," Miriam said, stretching the truth just a little.

When the call was over, predictably Miriam turned to Tom and asked why he and her father could never get on the same page. "You know my dad has so much business experience running his own company, Tom. Why are you fighting him on this?" Miriam asked impatiently.

"I could ask the same question. Why is he determined that we not sell Pellucid? Everyone on the board who owns shares is going to do very well from the sale. It doesn't make sense to me that we wouldn't seriously consider this opportunity. And who knows when the next mega-offer could come in? Do you want to work in the art gallery for the rest of your life?"

"As a matter of fact, yes, and if you weren't constantly at the office with Elise, you'd know that it means more to me than just a way to make a living," Miriam snapped angrily.

"Oh, my God, not this Elise issue again," Tom said, getting more annoyed by the minute. "We've been through this too many times! Elise is a member of my leadership team, and that's all."

"And she rides at the same stable!" Miriam retorted.

"But we often don't even ride at the same time. She has her own life too, Miriam," Tom said in an exasperated tone.

"Well, Daddy says that Elise—" Miriam started, and Tom cut her off.

"Your *father* has been commenting on Elise?" Tom said, incredulous. "He certainly has a lot to say about many things, most of which don't concern him!"

Tom smacked the pan on the granite countertop and opened the fridge.

"I'm suddenly not very hungry. I think I'll just go get ready for work and grab something on the way," Miriam said, turning her back.

"Fine by me," Tom replied as he strode out to the car, riding crop and helmet in hand. He hadn't meant to slam the front door.

"Another lovely morning at the Oliver home," Tom muttered as he pulled out of the driveway.

Chapter 7:

TOM—AUGUST 14

It took at least fifteen minutes behind the wheel of his beloved silver Porsche 911 Carrera for Tom to cool down from the exchange with Miriam. She certainly had a talent for setting him off lately, and his father-in-law was even more infuriating.

He and James had always been what Patrick called "sparring partners," with vastly different perspectives on just about everything, but it was getting worse with James trying to control Pellucid's operations. And the acquisition had become an inflection point for them both.

Tom had to admit that sometimes he did compare Miriam to Elise. Miriam was the perfect Southern sophisticate with a soft Carolinian accent that he found charming. But Tom couldn't help wishing that Miriam would be more reasonable to deal with and more interested in the business—like Elise—since, after all, Pellucid would be funding their financial future.

He realized, however, that it's never a good thing when you're in a relationship and wishing your partner could be more like someone else. So, he did his best to avoid such comparisons. Tom couldn't help feeling, though, that he enjoyed Elise's company much more than being at home, and he recognized that he had come to rely on Elise being there for him—both professionally and personally.

Driving west on Highway 401 with the sunroof open and music turned up, Tom started getting back into weekend mode. His annoyance faded as city warehouses and strip malls along the route gave way to farmers' fields and trees. Tom felt he could breathe again, and by the time he headed north to the Caledon stable, he was looking forward to seeing Titan and having a solo ride to clear his head.

The car handled beautifully, Tom noted, and he had no regrets about having splurged on the Porsche with some of the proceeds of his parents' estate. His brother had blown through his inheritance in no time of course and then resented Tom's purchase, calling it "another disgusting display of wealth."

Well, enough of that, Tom thought. *It's a sunny day; Titan is waiting, and things could always be worse.*

 *Chapter 8:*

TOM AND TITAN—AUGUST 14

T om turned onto the evergreen-lined laneway at the stable and saw his horse grazing contentedly in the field adjacent to the barn. As always, Titan came to the gate the instant he saw the car, which invariably made Tom's day. Perhaps surprisingly, horses get to know their owners' vehicles and recognize many distinguishing characteristics about their humans.

Tom led Titan into the barn and fastened him by his halter in the crossties for grooming. He saw that the staff had already finished mucking out the stalls and were probably off to the closest Tim Hortons coffee shop for a break. He had his "happy place" to himself.

Tom had bought Titan just before he founded Pellucid, and the horse was now twelve years old and in his prime. A classic, solid-black Friesian, Titan had an impressive build, standing 16.2 hands high at the withers—equating to five-feet-six-inches at the top of his shoulder.

When Titan had been brushed and saddled, Tom grabbed his GoPro from his tack box and mounted it on his helmet. A nervous flier, Tom kept a file of videos from his rides to watch at thirty-thousand-feet for a distraction. Focusing on

Titan got him through a lot of turbulence when he had to travel on business.

Competitive riders, especially those involved in horse trials, like to record their cross-country gallops and challenging jumps. At this stage in his life, Tom was content to record relaxing hacks in the countryside.

Tom was looking forward to his ride, and as a few more boarders were parking in the stable yard, Tom and Titan headed out to enjoy their usual route.

 *Chapter 9:*

THE ATTACKER—AUGUST 14

Protected from view by a canopy of trees, the attacker watched the horse and rider approaching as they followed the path at the edge of the cornfield. It wasn't hard to recognize that powerful black horse against the backdrop of light-colored corn stalks and intense blue sky.

There was no telling how well the plan would work. But the wire was now strung taut across the opening to the next field—about four inches off the ground where it could cause mayhem. It was a risky move, but the payoff could be worth it on so many levels. In fact, anything could happen. The horse could notice the wire and stop abruptly, jump the wire, or shy away—or even better, fail to see it and get entangled, trip, and fall. Whatever came next, the goal was for the horse to do the dirty work of dumping his rider onto the rocks at the side of the path.

If successful, it would be worth all the planning that had led up to this day: weeks of stalking this guy, using a drone to follow his favorite riding route, and figuring out access from the neighboring side road.

Today couldn't be more perfect for an "accident," and the moment was at hand.

Horse and rider were cresting the rise at the top of the field. Time to pull on a ski mask and gloves just in case and watch the action unfold.

Chapter 10

TOM AND TITAN—AUGUST 14

A s Tom and Titan began their ride, the sun was strong but a cool breeze rustled through the fields and Tom could tell that Titan was feeling lively. Tom moved the horse up into a trot along the familiar trail that traversed from the stable along the edge of the cornfield, through a break in the tree line into the hayfield, and down to the creek.

They were about to go through the gap into the hayfield when Tom felt Titan's muscles tense and saw the horse's ears prick up in the direction of the trees to the right. They had ridden here many times, so Titan's reaction seemed odd. *Maybe Titan is aware of a deer, or those nuisance wild turkeys concealed by the woods,* Tom thought. He took a firmer feel on the reins as he sat deeper in the saddle and slowed Titan to a walk.

Just then Tom noticed sunlight glinting off a wire stretched across the entrance to the next field. "What the hell is that?" Tom muttered. "Are you such a smart boy you saw it, Titan?"

Tom dismounted to have a look, taking off his helmet and tucking it under his arm while keeping a solid hold on the reins, as Titan continued to watch the woods intently. "Easy,

Titan, you're fine," he said, giving the horse a reassuring pat. Tom ran his free hand through his own hat-flattened hair and bent down to investigate the wire that had certainly never been there before. It was anchored to a sapling at the left side of the path.

"So some idiot deliberately placed this damned wire across the path at a height that would trip up a horse! Unbelievable!" Tom fumed aloud. Tom had heard of such things happening to ATV riders and snowmobilers with wires placed at chest level across trails, but this was a first.

With the shadows playing in the grass between the two fields, a wire placed so low to the ground could be hard to notice. Tom shuddered to think what would happen if a horse and rider were oblivious to the danger. Thin-gauge wire could slice a horse's leg right to the bone, so this was beyond infuriating.

Tom stood up and followed the wire to the right side of the path where rocks harvested from the field over many generations of farming had been shored up. He leaned forward to see how it was fastened, and as he did, a powerful blow from behind sent him to the ground with sudden and excruciating pain in his neck. Another blow, and all went black.

Tom had been struck with a jagged-edged rock and now lay crumpled next to the path.

The attacker then lashed out at Titan, striking the horse's shoulder with the rock and slashing the saddle while shouting, "Get out of here, stupid horse!"

Titan wheeled, freeing the reins from Tom's limp hand, and with stirrups flapping, took off for the safety of the barn. Horses being ridden on the trail whinnied to Titan as he galloped across the fields. Clearly, others were not far away.

———

Having only minutes to finish the job, the attacker positioned Tom's body on the stony ground with the bloody rock under his neck. Noticing a GoPro webcam attached to Tom's helmet, the attacker yanked it off and smashed it before replacing the helmet on Tom's head, leaving the strap undone as if the force of a fall had dislodged it.

Two nasty gashes at the base of Tom's skull leaked blood, clotting in his light brown hair, as the color quickly drained from his face. With riders approaching through the cornfield, the attacker stayed low to the ground while cutting and retrieving the wire. Deciding to grab the bashed GoPro in case the memory chip remained intact, the attacker scooped up the pieces and headed through the underbrush to a parked vehicle.

Driving away, the attacker was thinking what a touch of genius it had been to grab that rock. *What could look more natural? A perfect ending!*

Chapter 11:

ELISE AND TITAN—AUGUST 20

"A memorial service will be held tomorrow at Toronto's King Edward Hotel for thirty-eight-year-old Tom Oliver, CEO of Canadian data analytics company Pellucid and son of the late John Oliver, former Toronto chief of police. Tom Oliver died in hospital following an equestrian accident on August 14 in Caledon, Ontario, just northwest of the city. Named one of Canada's Top Forty Under Forty for 2020, Oliver founded Pellucid seven years ago. His company is considered a rising star in Canada's tech sector."

The radio announcer's voice on Toronto's all-news radio station droned on in the barn as Elise tried to steady herself against a stall door. It had all been surreal, starting with Titan's wild return to the barn, almost wiping out on the cement floor as he dashed crazily for his stall. The riders who found Tom and called 911 had returned to the stable in complete shock. And the next day there had been the horrible confirmation that Tom had died at the Orangeville hospital late that Saturday night.

Elise expected to see Tom stride into the barn at any moment for another ride on Titan—but that would never happen again.

He wasn't the first equestrian to have been killed in a freak accident, but it was nothing Elise could have imagined happening to an experienced rider like Tom. Judging from the scrapes on his saddle and the laceration on Titan's right shoulder, it seemed the horse had, for some reason, lost his footing on the rocks at the entrance to the field and gone down. Tom must have come off hard in just the wrong way.

It was especially upsetting to hear from the riders who found him that Tom's helmet wasn't fastened properly when he hit the rocks. Could he have undone the strap earlier because he was too warm? Did the latch snap open on impact even though it's designed not to? *If only he had been better protected,* Elise lamented. And if only she had come riding with him, perhaps she could have prevented this somehow. Instead, she was running errands downtown, oblivious to what was happening to Tom.

Now, all she could do for Tom was look after Titan, since Miriam certainly had no interest in the horse. And from what she was hearing about the memorial service, Miriam was more concerned with staging a successful social event than being bereft about losing her husband. *Maybe that isn't fair*, Elise admonished herself, *because everyone handles grief differently.* For her part, Elise couldn't have focused on planning an event and choosing a menu. In fact, she had scarcely eaten since Tom died.

Elise turned her attention to Titan and was thankful to see that the wound to his shoulder was healing nicely. Physically he would be fine with proper care, but his spirit might take longer. Titan's dark knowing eyes seemed to communicate a sense of loss that mirrored Elise's pain.

She and Titan shared the bond of having lost the person who had meant everything to them. Elise wrapped her arms around Titan's neck and buried her face in his thick mane as a wave of sadness washed over her. It had been almost a week since Tom's death, and she had no idea how to move forward without him—nor what would become of Pellucid.

 *Chapter 12:*

MIRIAM'S EVENT—AUGUST 21

Tom had shared with Miriam that when he died, he would never want his friends and family to be subjected to a depressing funeral service. He felt strongly about that after having suffered through his parents' double funeral following their car accident. Instead, he told her there should be a celebration of life with a party that he would have loved to attend. And no caskets or visitations—a simple cremation with his ashes strewn in a horse field would be just fine by him.

When considering where to have the memorial service for her husband, Miriam chose the Omni King Edward—a downtown Toronto landmark and classically elegant hotel. As she entered the second floor Vanity Fair Ballroom that Saturday prior to the midday event, Miriam knew it had been the right decision.

High above the ballroom, the elaborate recessed domed ceiling reflected the light emanating from elegant cascading crystal chandeliers. The supporting pillars topped with ornate sculpted filigree had stood strong since the hotel's inception in the early 1900s. Miriam thought her father would relate to the giant columns, reminiscent of Southern homes like the ones in Charleston, South Carolina, where they had often visited her grandparents when she was a child. Cognizant of the pandemic that only recently seemed to be easing off, Miriam had booked an oversized venue so guests could maintain extra personal space throughout the room.

Miriam had painstakingly selected a lunch buffet featuring a seafood station, pasta bar, traditional breakfast station with made-to-order omelets, massive charcuterie board with all manner of cheeses and cured meats, and in Tom's honor, a casual food station with pizza and classic Canadian poutine— fries covered in cheese curds and gravy. There was also a dessert station including Tom's favorite lemon tarts. Staff wearing masks and gloves would serve up the food, unlike pre-pandemic "help yourself" buffets.

The buffet was aligned under the domed ceiling, with four beverage stations adjacent to the ballroom walls offering peach Bellinis, Prosecco, and other wines and beers, plus coffee and tea options.

To ensure enough seating space for people to have a break from standing, Miriam arranged to have sleek white leather furniture placed around the perimeter of the room. Bouquets of white blossoms and greenery were also included in the staging, and an overwhelming number of flower arrangements from family and friends populated the ornate ballroom.

At the far end of the room, a table showcased photos from Tom's life. Starting with his youth in a Toronto suburb and culminating at his lovely home with Miriam, the photos told the story of Tom's progression through school and university in Toronto, attendance at the University of London for his master's in data science, and back to Canada to pursue his high-tech career.

There were photos of younger versions of Tom and Miriam when they dated in England fifteen years ago, posed in front of such London icons as Buckingham Palace, Hyde Park statues, double-decker buses, and the London Eye—the giant Ferris wheel dominating the view of the Thames.

And there were photos of their wedding, which had been held at the Pavilion at Angus Barn on the water near Raleigh, North Carolina. She'd had six bridesmaids in plum-colored silk gowns, and the venue was decorated with strings of tiny white lights that made the Pavilion magical in the evening. Tom had looked like a Hollywood star in his tuxedo, and it was a wedding to remember, she reminisced with a sigh.

There were also many photos of Tom's equestrian adventures, some showing him soaring over jumps during cross-country competitions in Caledon when he was younger. His riding photos as an adult were of him and Titan at the Caledon Hunt Club and riding Titan through the very fields where Tom had his terrible accident.

Miriam would have liked to display Tom's ashes in a lovely urn, but the hospital still hadn't released Tom's remains due to the COVID situation.

Instead, the photos will have to do, Miriam thought.

The overall effect of the ballroom staging was incredibly beautiful, and Miriam could not have been more pleased with the vision it would impart as attendees entered the room. Tom wouldn't have cared if it were fancy, but Miriam wanted it to be an impactful event.

As for her own presentation, Miriam was wearing a stunning black Gucci suit from Holt Renfrew, accessorized with her late mother's crystal butterfly pin. Her mahogany hair was pulled back and fastened into a messy bun for a classic look, with another simple but striking pin embellishing her chignon.

Everything must be absolutely perfect, Miriam thought, as she glanced in one of the ballroom's beveled mirrors. *Not that our marriage was perfect.*

But Miriam reflected that no one other than her father—in whom she had confided from time to time—had any idea about that.

Things had been great when she and Tom first married, but soon Tom's ambitious streak had him off and running. When he founded Pellucid, Miriam felt she had already lost a chunk of Tom to the business world, and when Elise came into the picture, she felt she was in danger of losing even more.

It's not that Elise did anything overt to capture Tom's attention—but she's obviously both beautiful and smart, Miriam thought. *And even worse, Elise and Tom seemed to be on the same wavelength all the time.*

Miriam had noticed their rapport at company social functions, and her father had made a few comments about the two of them as well.

Meanwhile, Miriam felt as if she and Tom had become more like roommates who shared household plans rather than spouses. She always had to negotiate with Tom to add a social event to his maxed-out schedule. He just hadn't cared enough about appearances and social standing, something she found infuriating.

When Miriam's dad asked her if she thought Tom was having an affair, she said dryly, "Not necessarily, unless you mean that he's sleeping with Pellucid 24/7." But she had shared her resentment of Elise and that she did have concerns about the relationship. Those concerns had been growing by leaps and bounds lately along with resentment of Elise.

She sighed, thinking she would never know if their marriage would have survived or if it was already a lost cause by the time Tom died. And she would never know if they might have had a child together. That was something she had never longed for, but she wondered if it might have strengthened their bond. So many unanswered questions.

Miriam was sad that her last interaction with Tom had been a fight about the acquisition and Elise. But even more, she felt angry that Tom had left her all alone—not to mention that his last gesture was slamming the front door.

Miriam glanced at her phone: it was time. She composed herself for the role of hostess she had been brought up to play so well. She saw her father, a tall, wiry sixty-one-year-old man with a shock of thick, graying hair, entering the ballroom wearing an impeccably tailored suit.

Chapter 13:

JAMES P. ROBINSON JR.

For a moment, seeing Miriam took James aback. She was the spitting image of his late wife, petite and understated, and it made him both extremely proud and nostalgic. He hurried over to see her.

"How are you holding up, my dear?" he asked as he kissed Miriam lightly on the cheek.

"I'm doing okay, thanks, under the circumstances. But I'm so glad you came. Thank you for being here for me, Daddy," she said, giving his hand a squeeze as she saw others approaching.

James P. Robinson Jr. was fond of tradition and proper presentation. So as Miriam suspected, he loved this stately old hotel where Tom's life would be celebrated. But Canadians on the whole struck James as too casual, lacking in decorum at times compared to the more genteel manners to which he was accustomed.

Imagine having a memorial service with no death certificate or remains, James scoffed to himself.

He understood that Miriam wanted to celebrate Tom's life, but the Canadian system seemed a complete shambles of irregularity in his opinion. However, this was a fine, classic event, and James was proud of Miriam.

It's too bad that Tom didn't seem to fully appreciate and cherish my daughter, as he should have, James thought bitterly.

He and Tom had certainly been cut from different cloth, agreeing to disagree on everything from politics to religion, to the part Tom should be playing in his marriage. It had worried James that Tom's liberal leanings could be a detriment to his own political ambitions in North Carolina where he was dedicated to the Republican Party and the Evangelical Christian church. It wouldn't do for his associates to know he was affiliated with a liberal who attended church only under duress.

James recalled having been enraged when Tom ridiculed Donald Trump for allegedly holding the Bible upside down in his staged photo op in front of Washington's St. John's Episcopal Church in June 2020. The two men usually tried to avoid clashing for Miriam's sake, but this time, Tom said that intelligent people needed to start calling out Trump for what he was: a white supremacist, autocratic, narcissistic, and highly subversive person in a position of ultimate power who used religion as a tool to advance his goals.

James had heard enough, and an ugly argument had ensued, culminating in James telling Tom they lived in two different universes. Tom had said it was no wonder, given that Fox News—the propaganda outlet fueling Trump's ambitions— was the center of the universe for James. Things had remained strained between them ever since.

The two of them also differed on how best to grow Pellucid, and James had been counting on a positive future for the company to fuel his political career. Now, with things up in the air and without Tom's backing, James hoped the sale would not go through so he would still have a leadership role to play.

After all, James was more than just Tom's father-in-law, "family and friends" round investor, and board member. As CEO of his own company in Raleigh, North Carolina, he had been an early adopter of Pellucid's technology, using its proprietary data-mining capabilities to maximize social media algorithms to influence consumer choices. Pellucid's latest program was proving invaluable, and James didn't want to lose that opportunity if Pellucid was acquired. The information was too powerful to give up.

He could now once again travel between Raleigh and Toronto, flying his small twin-engine plane, and he would be making the trip often to ensure the acquisition offer failed. He would focus his pressure on the "outside" board members who didn't hold leadership positions at Pellucid and could more easily be persuaded to vote against selling the company.

Chapter 14

PATRICK

W*ell, this certainly looks like an event Miriam would plan,* Patrick thought. He was amazed at the elaborateness of the never-ending brunch buffet and stylized decor. It was all Miriam and not so much Tom, though. And that was fine with Patrick.

At the end of the day, it's Miriam I'm here for, not Tom, Patrick thought, noting how pissed off he still was with Tom for how he had been treated.

How ironic that with all his prospects, this is what had befallen the man. Befallen: now that's an ironic choice of words under the circumstances, Patrick remarked to himself.

He glanced around the room and saw the Pellucid gang spread out throughout the gathering, lost and saddened without their fearless leader. *What a bunch, not one of them stuck up for me when I got the axe.*

Patrick would make his attendance short and sweet before heading to the classic hotel bar for some Irish whiskey instead of whatever corporate cocktails they were serving here. *Probably foppish Bellinis,* Patrick surmised with a smirk.

As he approached Miriam, he saw a flash of relief and welcome in her eyes, and Patrick gave her a generous hug reminiscent of their intimate moments at the last company party. It had felt good to move in on Tom's territory in whatever way he could.

When he took her hand and asked her, "Is there anything I can do?" he could see Miriam's brave facade almost give way to tears, but she held his hand tightly and shook her head.

Patrick could never quite figure out how Miriam and Tom had connected in the first place. Tom always said Miriam wasn't like other women he had dated and that her coy aloofness intrigued him. *I guess opposites attract*, Patrick thought, but he didn't think their marriage was standing the test of time. And Patrick had been doing his best to help that along.

Here comes that wanker Winston, Patrick thought as he realized it was time to let Miriam greet other guests. After a few inescapable pleasantries with Winston, he heard snippets of conversations happening around him.

Lawrence was saying, "Super guy—such a shame." Others commented, "So sad the horse went down in a rocky area like that," and "Tom will be missed." And it made Patrick feel all the more alive, and hungry, come to think of it.

Time to indulge in the buffet, Patrick decided.

Chapter 15

WINSTON

*W*ell, based on Patrick's body language, he's certainly not over Tom firing him, Winston thought.

Patrick's bold stance always made him look ready for a fight, but he had an added air of defiance today. When Winston greeted him, it took a nanosecond for Patrick to excuse himself.

Guess he can't be blamed for shunning the Pellucid team, but the whole situation was his own doing. If he had concentrated on his job instead of all the perks, things could have been much different, Winston thought, shaking his head.

As for himself, Winston was thanking God this was not a dismal funeral-home setting, because it was so much less depressing than those dreary places. Miriam had asked him to say a few words, and that would not be easy in any venue.

Winston had joined Pellucid a few years before and was Tom's right hand as chief financial officer. Now with Tom's passing, he had been named chairman and a co-CEO along with Elise in keeping with the terms of Pellucid's shareholder agreement. It was a lot to take on with the acquisition offer pending.

He had come to admire and respect Tom as a business leader and a great guy to hang out with. Tom had a strong work ethic but was happy to share a good bottle of wine or a Scotch after hours, seated in the leather chairs of the Pellucid office lounge. But Winston had concerns that Tom wasn't seeing the big picture of how important selling the company could be to all of them.

At this point, Winston was working harder than ever to demonstrate to Crystal Clere that Pellucid had ongoing value despite the loss of the company's CEO. Winston intended to see it through, given he was not foolish enough to walk away from millions of dollars. It's hard to ignore US $250 million, but it would take a delicate dance to ensure the offer stayed on the table. And to be honest, he realized he couldn't afford for the acquisition to fail.

For now, it was time for him to step up to the microphone and greet everyone. The formal part of the day would be very brief.

"Welcome, everyone, and thank you for coming out today to celebrate the life of Tom Oliver," Winston said. "Tom is—um, was—a man of distinction, a true leader in the tech community and the equestrian world. He will be sorely missed by all whose lives he touched, and his influence will live on. We are here to celebrate a life well lived by a good man who contributed much and whose further unrealized achievements are a true loss."

Winston looked around the room and saw their top investor, Lawrence Cameron, and his wife, Grace, chatting with Miriam and some of her key clients. Tom had indeed touched many lives that would never be the same again.

 *Chapter 16:*

LAWRENCE

L awrence and Grace Cameron had attended many events at the King Edward over the years and had even spent their wedding night there eighteen years prior. As Lawrence's second wife, Grace was the happy recipient of the success he had established before marrying her. She liked to tease him that their prenup agreement read like a section out of the US Constitution. *Well, a man has to do what a man has to do,* Lawrence thought.

Theirs had been a good union, and Grace had a knack for knowing exactly what was needed in each situation in their lives, be it keeping their two children on the straight and narrow, looking after their multiple residences, or supporting him at business events.

This event, although beautifully done, is such a very sad one, Lawrence thought. The last time he had seen Tom, he was full of life and ambition. Now Lawrence would never know for sure whether Tom would have decided to sell Pellucid. And the future of the company was less clear now that the driving force and visionary CEO was dead.

The business situation would have been much worse if Tom had not taken the bull by the horns and ousted Patrick

McGowan from the company. Lawrence would not have enjoyed dealing with a loose cannon like Patrick.

Lawrence reflected that having a soft heart was Tom's Achilles' heel, and he would have needed to cultivate a tougher edge. The same applied to dealings with his useless brother who was an albatross clinging to Tom for financial support.

It's important to look out for number one at all times— never mind all the bleeding-heart hangers-on, Lawrence noted to himself.

For his part, Lawrence had just been offered a lucrative deal from a US cable network to do investment commentary. Closing a major acquisition offer from a California tech company would be ideal to promote his personal brand south of the border. He hadn't disclosed that opportunity to Tom so as not to muddy the waters, but the acquisition would be a boon to Lawrence's career.

Lawrence would be sure to help Winston with due diligence for the acquisition before the upcoming board meeting and would align himself closely with Elise as well, who now had increased sway over the business, since she and Winston were interim co-CEOs.

Aside from all the business matters, Lawrence felt a sense of loss like he had never experienced before. He shuddered to think how horrible it would be to lose one of his own daughters if it was this hard to deal with Tom's passing. Grace must have sensed Lawrence was having a bad moment and slipped her arm through his, giving him a sideways squeeze to provide support at just the right time.

 *Chapter 17:*

ELISE

I really think I'm going to throw up, Elise thought as she fumbled with her bag and tried to figure out how to survive this memorial service. She was so incredibly heartbroken to lose Tom—both on a personal and professional level—that it made her physically ill. Finally, she had resorted to taking one of the relaxation pills the doctor had given her "in case of emergency" to slow her heart rate and avoid bursting into tears the minute she entered the ballroom.

As usual, heads turned when Elise arrived, although she was not aware. Elise wore a simple dark navy dress with a spaghetti-strapped top and pleated skirt and carried a matching bolero-cut jacket. With her blond hair cascading down her back in waves, she could have been modeling for an Omni Hotels promotion instead of attending a memorial for her kindred spirit. She made her way over to Miriam and expressed her condolences.

Miriam managed things seamlessly without a hint of emotion, thanking Elise for coming. "The ice maiden" was what always came to mind when Elise was around Miriam. The woman lacked warmth, and Elise couldn't fathom how

Tom's wife could be so different from his supportive and engaging personality.

Elise joined Winston, and as they stepped into a corner of the room, she struggled to maintain her composure. When she approached the photo array at the front of the ballroom, she couldn't hold it together any longer. Winston caught her as she started to falter and steered her to one of the white leather sofas.

Chapter 18:

MIRIAM

"As you know, Tom was taken before his time at only thirty-eight," Miriam said when it was her turn for remarks. "It's almost impossible to believe that he's gone, and I'm sure it feels like that to everyone. It's even harder because I didn't even get to see Tom at the hospital.

"Because of a COVID outbreak, I couldn't say a proper goodbye. I never dreamed I would ever have to part with someone I love on FaceTime."

Miriam struggled to swallow and continued.

"I hope you will all keep Tom in your hearts forever and cherish memories of your time spent together."

She caught Patrick's gaze from across the room and felt comforted by it. And it could have been her imagination, but she thought she saw Tom's detective friend, Jason Liu, in the outer mezzanine that was open to the lobby below.

How odd that he didn't join us, Miriam puzzled. The thought came and went quickly, because just then she noticed Tom's brother, Nate, in a far corner of the room looking incredibly out of place.

It gave her chills to see Nate because his resemblance to Tom was so striking. Both men were tall and slim with light brown hair, but whereas Tom had intense blue eyes, Nate had hazel eyes like his mother. And his rough lifestyle made Nate look older than Tom, even though he was four years younger.

Still, it was like seeing a ghost watching the proceedings unfold, and Miriam found it unsettling.

 *Chapter 19:*

NATE

The memorial service couldn't have been any more awkward for Nate. Everybody was aware that Tom was the shining star in his family, and Nate was the black sheep. As such, he knew his place—at the very back of the room, pretty much out of sight of the gathering.

Nate wasn't sure why he had come. After all, he and Tom weren't close, and Nate harbored a lot of animosity toward him. Nate didn't feel guilty, even about his last conversation with Tom before the accident. As he listened to the tributes, he recalled his final comment to his brother: "I'd be better off if you were dead. I'm sick of groveling while you enjoy the high life, so screw you!"

I meant that, and at least it was honest, Nate thought.

They had never been close, but the gap had widened when their parents died in the car accident right after Nate finished high school. Tom had left to study in London, despite the fact that meant Nate felt completely abandoned.

Guess getting out of town was Tom's way of dealing with things, Nate surmised.

Nate was supposed to start university that fall, but instead, he chose the school of hard knocks, hanging with a rough crowd and getting into drinking and drugs. He was more than aware it wasn't a stellar track record for the son of a former chief of police.

He had managed to pull himself out of the drug dependence early on, but the drinking was still very much a part of his life. He never had more than menial jobs and felt Tom owed him something because of his success, so he often guilted Tom into giving him money to support his habits. He was now faced with a sobering reality, with Tom dead and few prospects for himself on the horizon.

Well, I'll just have to get creative, he thought as he glanced around at all the successful and affluent people gathered in the room to honor his brother. And if he didn't miss his guess, his brother would have left him something substantial in his will, so that would do for now. In fact, he was counting on it.

Nate was glad to slip out as soon as the remarks were finished and leave them all to plunder the buffet.

 *Chapter 20:*

ELISE—AUGUST 23

As Elise walked from her condo to the office for the first time since Tom died, she was struggling to convince herself to be more focused on the business and to do a better job of moving forward without him.

It seemed to Elise that all the color had drained from her life. She was now living in a black-and-white world with only memories to cling to, instead of having her favorite person lighting up any room he entered. And in this desolate landscape, Elise felt like a hologram of herself going through the motions to simply function—not excited and passionate about work and life as she had been before losing Tom.

She realized it was already August 23, and the board meeting to ratify a new CEO and finalize the decision on the acquisition was slated for September 10 to ensure they could meet Crystal Clere's September 15 deadline. And it wouldn't be fair to expect Winston to carry the load by himself.

Winston had emailed her suggesting they plan to open the upcoming board meeting by replaying the Bloomberg TV interview with Tom, broadcast earlier in the summer. He thought the segment would remind the board of the company's trajectory and the reasons it was ripe for acquisition. When Elise got to the office, she decided to watch the video again to see if she agreed.

Elise poured a coffee in the kitchen and then set up her laptop in the main meeting room, selecting the interview from Pellucid's media coverage web page. With a single click, the video link popped up on the video wall. Elise hit Play and took a deep breath to prepare herself for seeing Tom on-screen.

"Hi, I'm Jillian Drew, and welcome to Top Market Moments. Today I'll be speaking with Tom Oliver, CEO of Pellucid, an emerging company in the big data and analytics technology space. Tom, thanks for joining us."

"Happy to be here, Jillian."

"Tom, since this is a new sector to many of our viewers, can you start by explaining big data?"

Elise had to press pause and take a moment before watching more of the interview. Tom had always lit up when he talked about Pellucid, and he flashed Jillian one of his charming, bright smiles. It was so hard to see Tom large as life, but she took a deep breath and hit Play once again.

"Absolutely. Now more than ever, massive amounts of information are being generated 24/7—a virtual tsunami of data referred to as big data. It's created from all sorts of digital interactions including internet searches, e-commerce data like retail sales and other financial transactions, and maybe most importantly, machine-to-machine internet of things sources."

"So how are businesses coping with the explosion of data?"

"That's a great question, Jillian. It's beyond overwhelming for companies to manage all the bits and bytes of data being generated. Typical data processing software tools are swamped just trying to track and process all that, let alone pull out key information that can help humans make smart decisions. So a major opportunity has emerged for companies like Pellucid to create software that can help address that challenge."

"Can you give us some examples of how or where big data analytics would be helpful?"

"Sure. Pretty much any organization across all industry sectors can benefit from this technology because it provides better insight to make informed decisions. An example would be a retail chain using analytics to find out what products are selling best and why customers are repeat buyers. Analytics has become even more critical during the pandemic given the spike in online shopping."

"That's pretty interesting stuff, but how does it work?"

"Now you're talking my language, Jillian." They both laugh as Tom continues. *"Data analytics is computer science-based and relies on detailed algorithms to do the detective work of extracting data and revealing patterns and trends."*

"You founded your company, Pellucid, seven years ago. Since then, has there been significant growth in your industry?"

"Yes, for sure. There's a growing list of companies in this field. Some are focused on machine data and data storage, others are involved in data mining—that's searches based on certain parameters—and

some specialize in data analysis. A number of big data players have gone public."

"Where does your company fit in the mix?"

"Pellucid is a growth-stage company in the middle of the pack, and we offer search technology that quickly extracts information and insights from large amounts of data. We chose the name Pellucid for the company because it means 'translucently clear,' shining light on things to make them easy to understand. We've been successful because Pellucid does data mining plus analytics, useful in multiple applications."

"For our investor audience, what do you think the prospects are for this technology in the future?"

"I would say the sky's the limit, but your viewers don't have to take my word for it," Tom smiles. "Top analyst firms are predicting that this will be a multibillion-dollar industry within the next five years. Some of the companies that have gone public in the data analytics space have seen strong spikes in their stock valuation, even during recent challenging economic times."

"What about Pellucid, Tom? Should we expect to see you announcing an IPO anytime soon?"

"I think every CEO dreams of taking an idea imagined over a coffee all the way through to a successful, publicly traded company. But that's something that unfolds over time, and only time will tell for Pellucid."

"Ha, being cagey on the IPO plans, I see! Well, thanks so much for spending time with us today, Tom, and shedding light on the burgeoning big data/analytics sector."

"Always a pleasure."

Elise hit Stop, and the frame froze on Tom's earnest and convincing face and those blue eyes. She always had an easy job coaching him for interviews and running through talking points because Tom was the ideal spokesperson. She had never met a journalist who didn't enjoy interviewing him.

Winston's proposal of using the interview as a starting point for the special meeting of the board was a good idea, Elise noted. It would be a good segue into discussion of the acquisition and whether it made sense for Pellucid to become part of Crystal Clere.

Crystal Clere was in the same type of business as Pellucid but with a broader scope, as it was a larger company involved with big players like Microsoft and Amazon. Pellucid would be a strategic addition to Crystal Clere's data-mining capabilities, helping them analyze metadata for their customers and potentially leveraging artificial intelligence.

But Elise understood that Tom might have been hesitant to sell because Pellucid would become a small cog in a much bigger wheel as part of Crystal Clere. He hadn't even told Elise how he planned to vote, so that would forever be an open question—although she was pretty sure he would have moved forward to sell Pellucid.

As Elise closed the video file, she wished she had more insight into how to put one foot in front of the other every day without Tom.

Elise remembered a dream she'd had the night before that seemed so real she could almost touch Tom. He was the only person who called her Ellie whenever the two of them were alone, and she had heard "Ellie, Ellie," over and over again. It felt as if Tom was desperately trying to tell her something she couldn't understand. She had awakened with a jolt in a cold sweat and cried herself back to sleep when she realized he couldn't possibly be there.

None of this was going to be easy, Elise thought sadly.

 *Chapter 21:*

THE READING OF THE WILL—AUGUST 25

Winston was aware that Tom had prepared his will a couple of years ago because they had discussed it over post-work drinks at the office one night. Tom had confided that Miriam thought it was a depressing topic and wanted nothing to do with it, so it had taken some convincing to get her to formulate her last wishes as well.

Tom had persisted, realizing that with a burgeoning business, significant investments because of his parents' life insurance policy, and his own savings, it was important to ensure that his assets would be allocated according to his wishes, not some government ruling.

Following Tom's passing, the law firm that drew up Tom's will—Elliott, Masters, Kline, and Duluthe—had contacted Winston to request that all beneficiaries be invited to attend a reading of the will at the Pellucid office.

Today, the group of beneficiaries was gathered in Pellucid's meeting room for the reading including Miriam, Nate, Elise, and Winston. The only one missing was Patrick, who had not too politely declined when Winston extended the invitation to attend.

The presenting lawyer, Stephen Masters, started by saying how sorry he was for Miriam's loss and everyone else's sadness. He explained that he would take everyone through the allocations within the will and noted that the average estate requires up to a year and a half to administer, the last step in the process being the transfer of assets to beneficiaries.

Masters also acknowledged that a will reading is highly unusual in modern times. But it was Tom's instruction that his will be read to all affected parties as a group so that everyone would have full visibility to his decisions. Tom abhorred any controversy over money and was adamant about having a formal reading.

Masters then noted that people are typically worth more dead than alive in terms of finances and that, indeed, Tom had left those dear to him well protected through insurance and bequests.

Geez, I guess "worth more dead than alive" passes for lawyerly wit at a time like this, Winston thought, raising his eyebrows as Elise glanced his way. For his part, Winston had no idea why he was included in the reading of the will.

Masters indicated that, as with most married couples, the matrimonial home being in both names was entirely Miriam's upon his death—and they had mortgage insurance, so the house was now paid in full. Tom also had considerable investments outside the company in his retirement savings that were also transferring to Miriam.

Looking at Miriam with a kind smile, Masters said Tom had expressed concern that a sports car would be dangerous for her. So, he left his fun ride—the Porsche 911—to his CFO, Winston.

Winston was shocked but maintained his inscrutable demeanor. But behind the facade he was overwhelmed with guilt, while at the same time wishing that the whole process of the will allocations could be faster than the year Masters had mentioned.

Masters continued, saying that to his brother, Nate, Tom left a sizeable trust fund. The trust, which came primarily from Tom's well-invested life insurance money from their parents' passing, would be managed by the legal firm.

The condition attached to the trust fund was that it would be reassigned to charity with no further claim to be entertained from Nate if ever Nate approached any of the other beneficiaries for money, or if he ever tried to tap into the proceeds from Pellucid or any of its derivatives or affiliates.

Very clever of Tom, Winston thought. *The trust will dole out a decent living but not enable Nate to take out chunks of cash and run through the proceeds. So Tom ensured Nate's security and perhaps decent behavior too.*

Winston stole a glance at Nate, who looked relieved but angry at having been "managed" so carefully by his older brother.

To his former colleague Patrick, Tom left his considerable Scotch collection, including Islay malts, Speyside and Highland selections, and some top-flight Irish whiskeys too. There were even a couple of single-malt selections from distilleries in Japan and India. Patrick and Tom had often enjoyed Scotch tastings and indulged in the odd cigar, before the firing.

In closing, Masters said the will allocated significant funds to keep Tom's horse, Titan, well looked after for many years, with the allocation entrusted to Elise to whom he bequeathed Titan and his horse tack. At that, Winston noticed Miriam's face harden into a terse expression.

———

You've got to be kidding me! Miriam fumed to herself. *That will keep the damn horse happy and then some*!

Miriam considered the funds to be highly excessive and suspected the intent was to ensure that Elise was well looked after too. With this parting gesture from Tom, she concluded that she had her answer as to what would have happened between them had he not died.

Will reading is done and I'm livid! Miriam texted to the absent Patrick.

Oh, I'm sorry to hear that, Patrick texted back.

Maybe you can come by Friday afternoon so I can update you? Miriam texted.

Of course.

 *Chapter 22:*

ELISE—AUGUST 25

A t the end of the meeting, the presiding lawyer approached Elise and asked her if they could talk privately in her office. When she had closed the door, Masters spoke quietly as he confided that Tom had given him the key to a safe deposit box at the downtown TD Canada Trust Centre on King Street West, along with a signed letter of permission granting Elise access should anything happen to him.

Tom had given specific instructions that Masters should give the key to Elise. No one else, only Elise. Masters had no information as to what it would reveal, just that Tom said, "It will make sense to her."

Elise found herself commenting that nothing made sense to her, especially why someone like Tom had to die. As Elise struggled to hold back tears, Masters said gently that perhaps the contents of the safe deposit box could bring some comfort.

Miriam was coming down the hallway as Elise and Masters stepped out of the office, and Miriam gave Elise an icy stare. Elise couldn't wait for all this to be over; it was so painful having to deal with everything involved with Tom being gone.

And Miriam's attitude toward me is so unnecessary and just adds to the angst, she thought miserably.

Elise spent the minimum time necessary to be polite, sharing a light lunch served in the boardroom with Masters and the other beneficiaries and then excusing herself to face the next reality of whatever Tom had tucked away for her eyes only.

It was about a fifteen-minute walk from the Pellucid office to the bank, and as she hurried along downtown sidewalks, Elise mulled over what could possibly need such secrecy or be so important to him. Tom had never mentioned anything to her about it, so she had absolutely no idea what could be in the safe deposit box. She was still absorbing the terms of Tom's will that left her such a generous allocation to look after Titan, and now this was an added twist.

When Elise entered the bank's expansive main floor and identified herself at reception, she was escorted to the safe deposit vault one level below. In the rows of multi-sized boxes, Tom's was one of the many smaller ones ideal for storing paperwork.

Elise took the box into a small cubicle where she could review the contents privately. She felt some trepidation and found herself holding her breath as she lifted the lid.

Inside, Elise found an envelope with her name on it, in Tom's handwriting. She traced the letters with her fingertips, realizing she would never hear Tom say her name aloud again. She took a moment to contain her emotions and opened the letter. It read:

Dear Ellie,

If you're reading this note, it means that I'm incapacitated or worse, so I'm sorry for whatever circumstance has brought you here, but I wanted you to have access to my personal files. You're the only one who will appreciate what they mean to me. This is a bit surreal because I'm planning for something

*that may never happen. (I guess everyone hopes that
when they plan for the worst.)*

*My files are on the computer in my office, and
here is my password: Titan542!. There is a second
layer of file protection, and the password to that is
$Grange5378. If anything happens that my com-
puter is inaccessible, you can also download files
from the cloud using those passwords.*

*You know how important you are to me, but
let me just say that you are, and always will be, my
person. Please take good care of yourself, and I wish
you nothing but the best, always!*
Much love,
Tom

Elise sat in the silent, oak-lined cubicle and reread the
letter several times. Although she knew they had a close relationship, it was a special gift to her that Tom had called her his
"person" and signed "much love." She would cherish those
affirmations forever.

Elise took some time to compose herself before tucking
the letter into her bag and returning the box to its slot among
so many other such boxes holding who knows what secrets.
She passed by the immense vault door that served as the gate-
keeper to the safe deposit boxes and went back up the escalator
to the main floor.

She was struck by the fact that the bank had beautiful
vases of yellow chrysanthemums placed throughout the open-
concept main floor, a welcome human touch in this historical
bank. The flowers sparked a bittersweet memory of Tom, when
he had brought her a lovely bouquet of yellow and white roses
as a thank-you after a successful marketing launch.

Elise walked back to the Pellucid office and planned to
stay late to ensure she would be the only person still on site.

 *Chapter 23:*

ELISE AND DISCOVERIES—AUGUST 25

Elise looked out Pellucid's lounge windows to the street below. It was almost eleven o'clock, and the city lights shimmered on this cool and cloudless night.

The building was eerily quiet as Elise headed down the hallway to Tom's office. Being in his space, she could still detect the faint scent of his cologne and felt overwhelmed with memories of many hours spent here working on Pellucid marketing and product launch plans.

But it was a comfort to be surrounded by his familiar things as if nothing had changed and he could come back at any moment. His office was just as he left it since she and Winston had not yet wanted to face the task of sorting his effects. And with the focus on prepping for the upcoming board meeting, there had been no time.

She settled herself in Tom's chair and turned on his computer, tense about what she might find. Her fingers were shaking as her nerves kicked in, so she painstakingly entered the passwords that safeguarded Tom's personal files.

When the files popped up on the screen, Elise exhaled with relief when she discovered that the big secret was numerous videos of Tom's rides on Titan.

They were all dated and labeled with Tom's impressions of how the rides had gone, like, "Big jump into the creek" or "Lovely gallop through hayfield." He had put a summary note indicating that these were his sanity savers when he encountered turbulence when flying. Elise had realized that Tom was a nervous flyer only when they were on a business trip to California the previous year and he had clutched her hand tightly during a bumpy descent.

Along with the video files, Elise found a Word file noting how Tom had captured the videos using a Bluetooth-enabled GoPro that could be controlled remotely with an app on his smartphone. Videos could auto-upload both to his computer and the cloud.

Elise always thought the GoPro memory chip was required to enable saving video files, but Tom's system was automatic.

Trust a computer science guy to have that figured out, Elise thought.

She stopped short at a video titled, "Ellie." It was a video his helmet-cam had recorded when they'd returned from a ride. She remembered the day, when Tom had caught a mouse by the tail and chased her with it like a teenager. The video showed her squealing and running into the storage shed where she was cornered.

Laughing and winded, she leaned on hay bales, flushed and with her hair tumbling onto her shoulders. Tom had commented that she was beautiful, and then turned and released the mouse outside to escape the barn cats. The memory made her smile for the first time in days.

But then Elise felt as if her heart almost stopped when she saw an untitled video dated August 14, the day Tom died. She could barely breathe.

Elise realized that Tom must have been wearing the GoPro when he rode that day. She didn't remember anyone saying anything about the helmet-cam when Tom was found. So that seemed odd, but clearly the video from his ride should be automatically downloadable from the cloud.

Did she want to replay the video of a horrible accident? Or would it even have been recorded, given his fall?

She decided she couldn't avoid facing reality. Elise retrieved the video and hit Play.

The footage started with a typical ride down the path leading from the barn to the cornfield. But as Tom and Titan approached the gap to the next field, Titan stopped moving. The video shook when Tom obviously dismounted. Elise heard him say that someone had strung wire across the gap, and she could see the wire clearly on the video. From his tone of voice, Elise could tell he was angry—and with good reason.

The video went wonky because Tom must have taken his helmet off and tucked it under his arm, so she saw part of his shirt and Titan's head positioned sideways on the video. She heard Tom reassure Titan, and there was movement as he presumably checked out the wire. Suddenly Tom cried out like he had been hurt. The camera hit the ground and all she could see was dirt and grass.

Then what she saw was so disturbing: someone picked up the helmet! The video was blurry, but she could see that the GoPro had been grabbed by a person wearing a ski mask, and then the screen had gone black.

"Oh, my God! Oh, my God!" Elise exclaimed. She was horrified and clasped her hands over her mouth in shock.

Elise found herself staring at the computer in stunned silence. She could scarcely believe what the video revealed, it was so surreal and unimaginable. Could someone have deliberately sabotaged the path and then attacked Tom? Not only that, had they been careful enough to try to cover their tracks by taking the GoPro? And who was the monster in a balaclava who had done this?

She replayed the video several times. It was evident that Tom had dismounted, so he certainly didn't fall off Titan. And it was obvious that Titan's injury wasn't from losing his footing.

The wire and the fleeting view of a possible attacker made it unavoidable for Elise to conclude that this was murder.

She shivered with the realization. And then Elise put her head in her hands and cried, realizing how awful it must have been for Tom and how his life had been cut short for no reason. And she was angry—so angry that someone could do such a thing! *Who would do this? And why?*

After the initial shock had passed, Elise went to the office kitchen and pulled a bottle of white wine from the fridge. Her hands shook so much she could barely pour herself a glass. Returning to Tom's office, she contemplated what to do.

If she went to the police with a disjointed video, would they think her delusional, or would they take it seriously and investigate?

Should she confide in someone to get a second opinion before going to the police?

She couldn't discuss this with Miriam because it would just upset her, and anyway, she didn't feel close enough to Miriam to broach the topic. *Miriam probably doesn't even know that Tom had a GoPro because she wasn't the least bit interested in his riding.* In fact, Elise suspected Miriam resented his time at the barn.

In days gone by, Elise might have confided in Patrick, but after recent events, that would be uncomfortable. And Elise was already wary that Patrick might somehow try to get back into Pellucid now that Tom was gone, so best not to muddy the waters.

Elise decided the most logical thing to do would be to check out the scene of the accident, however painful that would be, before involving anyone else. If any evidence of foul play remained, she would find it. *That might make a stronger impression on the police*, she thought.

Elise closed out of the computer, careful to ensure that Tom's files remained safely stored. She then texted Winston that she would be out of the office the next day and headed home.

Chapter 24:

ELISE AT THE SCENE—AUGUST 26

When she arrived at the barn the next morning, Elise was happy to hear from the barn manager that the vet had been out and advised that Titan could start doing light work. A sedate ride would be good for him to get his muscles moving.

Elise went out to the field where Cadette, the horse she part-boards, was turned out. She gave her girl carrots and pats and a promise to come back for a ride soon. Then she brought Titan into the barn and prepped for their ride. Titan appreciated being groomed and when she rubbed the currycomb in circular motions on his neck, he turned his head and rested it on her shoulder.

"You're such a sweet boy, Titan," Elise told him, patting him and kissing his velvety-soft nose. She finished tacking up, and they were ready to head out.

It had rained the last two days, and Elise was doubtful of finding any evidence of Tom's murder, but it was worth a try. She and Titan followed the fateful route that Tom had taken and soon approached the entrance to the hayfield where the attack took place.

Titan was traumatized by what had happened, and he balked at going close to the opening, paying extra attention to the wooded area to the right of the path. With Titan starting to prance on the spot, Elise decided this wasn't the best idea on her part and she turned Titan back toward the stable.

Once Titan was grazing contentedly in his paddock, Elise changed her boots and borrowed the stable's ATV to drive back to the scene. She parked at the edge of the field and went to inspect things on foot. It was good she had put on her rubber paddock boots, because the ground was mucky.

Examining the base of the trees she had seen in the video, Elise could see that the bark was chafed at the height where the wire had been fastened. But there was no wire remaining and any footprints, had they been left by the attacker, were now mired in mud. She then made her way through the underbrush on the right side of the clearing, and it was evident that someone had cut back some of the growth to make an easier approach. Farther from the hayfield, the woods thinned to a right-of-way at the edge of a side road, which would have provided easy access and escape for the attacker.

This must have been preplanned and carefully orchestrated, Elise concluded. The idea that the killer was still at large somewhere was chilling. It was time to contact the police and share the video.

 *Chapter 25:*

ELISE AND PATRICK—AUGUST 26

As Elise got back to the barn, she almost ran into Patrick with the ATV. Patrick seemed to have come out of nowhere just as she rounded the corner of the stable. Fortunately, he had heard her coming so didn't step into her path.

"Hey, Elise, are you trying to do me in?" he asked wryly as Elise stepped down from the four-wheeler.

"Sorry about that," Elise said.

"No worries," Patrick said, looking uncomfortable at having encountered her at the barn. "What are you doing here on a workday anyway? And on an ATV, no less?"

"Oh, I was just checking something, nothing major," Elise said, trying to sound nonchalant.

"That makes zero sense, Elise. Try again," Patrick said impatiently.

Elise had no desire to start a row with Patrick, so she told part of the truth.

"Well, honestly, I felt compelled to go to the field where Tom died. And Titan was hyper going back there, so I took the ATV," she said.

"Why on earth would you want to do that?" Patrick persisted.

"I just wanted to see for myself that it was possible for an accident to happen in that particular spot. I mean, you know what a good rider Tom was," Elise said, trying to cover up her real intentions.

"Yes, but how could it be anything but an accident? You're not thinking there was some kind of foul play?" Patrick said.

"I don't know. It's all so unbelievable," Elise responded. "I don't know what to think."

"If you ask me, you're just grasping at straws. You need to accept that Tom is dead, period," Patrick said curtly. "Your problem is you were in love with the man, am I right?"

Elise felt her face getting hot and ignored his comment.

"Like everyone, Patrick, I'm coping the best I can. And what are you doing here? Slacking off from your new job?" Elise said, desperately trying to change the subject but coming off as judgmental.

"First of all, my schedule is no longer any of your business. Second, suggesting that Tom's death could be anything but an accident is ridiculous, and you would just upset Miriam with that kind of nonsense. And if you must know, I'm here to help the girls build a pen for that ugly potbellied pig they bought. Damn thing keeps getting out and scaring the horses," Patrick said.

"That's nice of you to help out, Patrick. Sorry, but I have to run," Elise said as she abruptly turned away and walked quickly to her car to escape more conversation.

Elise got in the car and immediately admonished herself for the interaction with Patrick.

How could I have been so loose-lipped with him, of all people! she chided herself. *How many times have I given spokespeople a standby statement like, "We don't comment on rumor and speculation" to avoid oversharing information with the media? And then I blurt out the possibility of Tom's death not being accidental! What terrible luck to run into Patrick here!*

Patrick had certainly caught her off-guard with no alternate explanation for being out on the ATV. But at least she hadn't spoken the word *murder*.

Seeing him reminded Elise of the tense atmosphere at Pellucid when Patrick had known the axe was coming and he was livid with Tom. Her intuition was telling her that Patrick's involvement with Pellucid was not over, even though she had heard he landed a new role with a small tech company. Elise so wished she had not encountered him here today.

That night, Elise dreamed again, and this time she replayed the video of Tom with the mouse. But instead of laughing and joking, Tom suddenly got serious and tried to tell her something.

Again the image faded, and she was left feeling empty, alone, and frustrated that she couldn't tie everything together. Titan appeared in the dream, nuzzling her to comfort her, and she woke up with her arms outstretched as if around the horse's neck. And Elise wondered if she would ever feel whole again.

PART TWO

 *Chapter 26:*

TOM—*DAY 1*—AUGUST 14

he EMTs had managed to stop the bleeding from two big gashes on the man's neck before loading him on a stretcher into the ambulance. They'd had a hell of a time getting the portable Stryker stretcher from the side road through the patch of woods to where he lay crumpled on the rocks. When the 911 call came in, they were told he had taken a bad fall off his horse, and that was an understatement given his injuries.

He must be one hardy guy, though, because he was regaining consciousness already.

"Hey there," an EMT said to Tom.

"Hi. Where am I?"

"You're in an ambulance. You took a fall but you're going to be fine. Just try to relax," the EMT said reassuringly.

Tom's neck was excruciatingly painful, his head hurt, and objects in the ambulance were sometimes floating in the air. The EMT's face was going in and out of focus.

"No, I didn't," Tom said. "I didn't fall off. My horse I mean. I was attacked," Tom said.

The EMT was skeptical and said, "Look, can you tell me what day it is?"

"August 14."

"And what's your name?" the EMT asked.

"Tom Oliver."

"Tom, how were you attacked?"

"There was a boobytrap—I, I think they must have struck me with something. Look at my GoPro."

"Okay, I will let the police know, and they'll get to the bottom of this. Right now, you need to stay calm," the EMT advised.

"Detective Liu. Toronto Police. Get Detective Liu—Toronto Police," Tom managed to say before everything went black again.

Chapter 27:

DETECTIVE LIU—*DAY 1*—AUGUST 14

I t had been a quiet Saturday at the Ontario Provincial Police office in the Town of Orangeville with a few traffic infractions and one person intoxicated in a public place: in other words, the usual. That is until they got a call from the Orangeville hospital saying that a man who was thought to have had a serious horseback riding accident was claiming to have been attacked.

The alleged victim, whom they had determined was from Toronto, asked that they specifically contact a Detective Liu on the Toronto Police Service.

The on-duty OPP officer called central dispatch in Toronto to track down Liu. He was in luck: Detective Jason Liu worked out of headquarters and was on duty this weekend.

"Hey, Detective. It's Officer Brett from the Orangeville OPP detachment. How are you?"

"Good, thanks. How can I help?"

"We've had a report from the Orangeville hospital that a guy named Tom Oliver is in emerg with serious lacerations to his neck and possible concussion. He was reported to have fallen off his horse in Caledon, but he claims he was attacked by a perp. For whatever reason he asked that you be notified.

We figured rather than starting an investigation, we'd connect with you first."

"I appreciate that, Officer Brett. I know who he is. He's CEO of a company that's worth considerable coin, and he recently reported that someone almost ran him over in Yorkville. It was a clear day, no reason for a vehicle to jump the curb. He also said he had been followed on multiple occasions recently. I've got a general occurrence report on file from the Yorkville incident, and I'm not liking the probability that someone wants him dead."

"Since you have an open case with this guy, how do you want to handle things, Detective?"

"I'd like to take lead on this, but I'd appreciate your help. Can you post plainclothes with him? Assuming he doesn't have surgery, it probably means putting an officer outside his room for the duration. I'll head up to Orangeville right away."

"Sure, that's not a problem. Just so you're aware, visiting at the hospital is restricted at the moment because of a COVID variant outbreak, so only essential workers are allowed in. They'll have you wear PPE, the whole nine yards."

"Oh, man, I was hoping we were done with that! Thanks for letting me know. So, Officer Brett, as far as next of kin is concerned, can you notify Tom's wife that he has been injured but make sure no one has access to him besides medical personnel? That should be easy to pull off given the COVID situation," Liu said.

"You got it, Detective. Meanwhile, our guys can go to the incident scene and check it out," Officer Brett responded.

"Meet me at the hospital whenever you have more information?" Liu added.

"Roger that."

When Liu got off the phone with Orangeville OPP, his next call was to his commanding officer, and then they jointly spoke with their chief of police. Since Tom was the son of a former police chief, a legendary figure on the force, this would be a special case. Liu had the full endorsement of the current police chief to do whatever was required to keep Tom from further harm.

 *Chapter 28:*

LIU INVESTIGATES—*DAY 1*—AUGUST 14

It was about an hour's drive from his office in downtown Toronto to Orangeville—at least on a Saturday when workday commuters weren't on the road—and Liu made even better time.

When Liu arrived at the hospital, he found Tom had already been triaged and moved to a private room. Orangeville OPP had an officer on duty outside Tom's room, dressed in civilian clothes to avert attention as requested.

Liu met with the neurologist who had fortunately been on call that Saturday and who had been directing Tom's care. The neurologist advised Liu that scans indicated Tom was a lucky man, escaping immediate death by mere centimeters. He doubted that the injuries had been sustained in a fall off a horse given the angle and depth of the wounds, supporting Tom's claim of an attack. The injuries were more indicative of deliberate blunt force trauma.

The reports showed no brain bleed, so there shouldn't be any brain swelling or risk of stroke, the doctor explained. Tom was also fortunate not to have a skull fracture, as both blows had struck his neck just below the skull. The cuts were deep but didn't sever muscles or fracture any vertebrae, which could have put him at risk for nerve channel or carotid artery damage.

"If this guy was a cat with nine lives, he would have just used up ten of them," the neurologist told Liu.

With the bleeding abated on site by the ambulance EMTs and the gashes mitigated by the trauma team, Tom's prospects for a full recovery were good, the neurologist reported. However, because of the reverberating effect of the impact on his neck, the doctor advised that Tom would likely have symptoms similar to a concussion for some time, including nausea, unsteadiness, and headaches. Keeping the lights low, avoiding reading and screen time, and lots of rest would be the best formula for recovery, along with some serious pain meds.

Liu asked the doctor if he could speak with Tom and was advised that he should keep the conversation short and not push too hard for information.

Meanwhile, Officer Brett reported OPP had found little physical evidence at the site of the accident but did find footprints in the woods adjacent to the site and tire tracks in the soft shoulder of the side road. The EMT had mentioned a GoPro, but they didn't find it on site. However, some bits of plastic found on the scene had been sent to the forensics lab for analysis.

Liu opened the door to Tom's room and began the next phase of his investigation.

Chapter 29:

LIU AND TOM—*DAY 1*—AUGUST 14

The pale man lying in the hospital bed with a dark bruise on his right cheekbone and intravenous tubes leading off his right hand bore little resemblance to his dynamic friend, Liu noted. Tom had come close to dying in this incident, and Liu would make damn sure there wasn't another attempt on his life.

Liu moved a chair close to the bed and said, "Hey, Tom."

Tom opened his eyes, and it took him a moment to focus.

"Hey, Jason," Tom said, giving a weak smile.

"How are you doing?" Liu asked.

"I've been better," Tom responded.

Liu was relieved that Tom was lucid, able to recognize him despite his COVID mask, and cognizant even on pain meds—which was very important for what he was about to propose.

"Can you tell me what happened?" Liu asked.

"I was out riding, and someone had strung a wire across the path into the next field. When I got off Titan to have a look, I think someone nailed me in the back of the neck," Tom said. "That's all I know."

"Tom, I'm very concerned for your safety. Do you remember the incident in Yorkville?" Lui asked.

Tom gave a slight nod and winced from the pain.

The detective continued. "And you weren't entirely sure it was an attempt on your life. But this situation leaves no doubt in my mind that someone is out to get you. The next time, you might not be so lucky. We don't have a lot to go on. Orangeville OPP only found a couple of minor things to look into from today's attack," he added. "You and I talked about the motivation for someone coming after you, and I'll need to investigate possibilities. But that takes time, and in the meantime, you're at risk. Are you with me so far, Tom?"

"Yes, I'm with you," Tom replied, as he touched his slightly swollen forehead.

"I'll cut to the chase. I'd like to take you out of action for a while and see if anything surfaces," Liu said.

"What does that mean?" Tom asked, his voice getting weaker.

"We'll declare you dead and move you to a safe house," Liu replied.

"What about Miriam, my coworkers?" Tom asked, his headache no doubt worsening.

"I know it seems cruel to deceive people close to you, but we don't know at this point who is involved in this. That makes everyone a suspect. And if the attacker learns you're still alive, chances are there will be another attempt on your life," Liu said.

Tom frowned but didn't respond.

"Think about it, Tom. You're in a unique position given that you have very few people in your immediate family circle—only Miriam and Nate. It will be hard on them, but then it will be a major relief when you reappear after we have more insight on the attempted murder."

"So how would this work?" Tom asked.

"Our legal team needs you to sign a form giving consent to enter a safe house under the protection of the Toronto Police Service. The neurologist can witness that you're of sound mind and that you gave consent freely.

"The safe house is in downtown Toronto and we'll need you to stay there, having zero contact with the outside world, while we conduct the investigation.

"We have a doctor from St. Michael's Hospital who works with us regularly on such cases, and he'll look after you. The house will be under our watch 24/7. It's easier for us to guarantee your safety in a set location rather than with you out in the community as usual," Liu explained.

"How do you fake my death? What about a body?" Tom said.

"I'll ask your neurologist if he's amenable to giving you extra sedation later today if needed to make this look convincing. We'll connect with Miriam on FaceTime to notify her of your passing and show you in the hospital bed. She can't come here anyway because there's a COVID outbreak. The coroner's office will be notified of an exception to issuing the death certificate."

"That's going to be awful for everyone! So I can't even let Miriam and Elise know?" Tom asked, seeming alarmed.

"Who is Elise?"

"She's on my team at Pellucid," Tom said.

"No, it's all or nothing on these things. It's the only secure way, Tom," Liu said firmly.

Tom relented only after Liu argued it was absolutely necessary to fake his death in order to protect him, and that in the long run, this was the right thing to do for both Tom's family and for his company. Tom signed the consent form before falling asleep thanks to his medications.

Miriam was advised that Tom's condition was worsening, and late that night she was told he had passed away and witnessed his "body" on FaceTime.

The Toronto Police used an ambulance service to remove Tom from the hospital, transferring him to a sedan in Georgetown before continuing to the safe house, where he arrived at one o'clock Sunday morning, officially dead—and no doubt feeling authentically close to it.

Dr. Mark Anderson from St. Michael's Hospital met them at the safe house and would spend the night monitoring Tom. He would be off duty at the hospital the next day, so he assured Liu he would keep an eye on Tom all day Sunday to make sure he had his meds and to watch for anything concerning. He advised it would be important, with Tom off intravenous fluids, for him to start eating and drinking normally, and for his headaches to lessen.

They would know by Sunday night if there would be any complications.

 *Chapter 30:*

TOM AND DR. ANDERSON—*DAY 3*—AUGUST 16

om awoke to light filtering through the curtains in his room, and he quickly closed his eyes as the brightness set off a headache. At least the headaches were easing off some, and he had been able to eat soup the previous night. He had also navigated the hall to the bathroom in the night without feeling dizzy and having to use the wall for support.

When he reopened his eyes, he saw Dr. Anderson coming in to check on him again.

What a great guy, Tom thought. He had been at the safe house nonstop, and Tom had appreciated the care and the company.

"Hey, Tom, Florence Nightingale again to see you," Dr. Anderson joked. "I'm just going to give your heart a listen and take your blood pressure. I'm sure you know the drill by now."

Tom nodded and was immediately sorry he'd moved his neck. "I hope I get some of those pills again too?"

"Ha, yes, you're due for another set of painkillers for sure, Tom. And after we change the dressing on your neck, we'll see if you can manage some breakfast," Dr. Anderson said, as he slipped Tom's bruised arm into the blood pressure sleeve.

The incident had happened Saturday morning and now on Monday things were going well. Tom was pleased that Dr. Anderson expressed confidence in a full recovery from the vicious attack, given that his concussion-like symptoms were improving and wounds had started to heal.

"So, Doc, when do you think my vision will get back to normal so I can read or watch TV?" Tom asked.

"Oh, you need to give it at least another day or so, Tom. You rush it, and you'll just delay your recovery," Dr. Anderson warned. "You shouldn't use your computer or watch TV at all, and I'd suggest limiting time spent reading until your symptoms have completely subsided."

"Oh great. I may actually die—of boredom! At some point I hope to at least be able to watch some of my riding videos for something to do," Tom said.

"Tom, that reminds me. Detective Liu wanted me to ask you about a GoPro of some kind you use when you're riding," Dr. Anderson said.

"Yes, did the police find it?" Tom asked, intrigued.

"No, they didn't. Are you sure you had it that day?" Dr. Anderson said.

"Absolutely!" Tom said, looking puzzled.

"Tell Liu he doesn't need the actual GoPro to access the video. I have it set up so it records via my phone to cloud storage, so I'll be able to find it—if and when you two let me have a computer again," Tom said hopefully.

"Nice try, and not today," Dr. Anderson said. "But soon."

Dr. Anderson said he would be returning to his regular duties at the hospital that night, but told Tom he would continue to stop by intermittently to check on him for the next couple of days.

Chapter 31:

LIU AND TOM—*DAY 5*—AUGUST 18

Detective Liu was intrigued when Dr. Anderson informed him that video of the attack might be accessible—even without locating Tom's GoPro. Dr. Anderson had now given his approval for Tom to go online and retrieve it, and Liu was keen to view the footage. The detective dropped everything and went to the safe house to watch it with Tom, hoping that either the recording would be revealing or that it might prompt Tom to remember more about the attack.

The outcome was disappointing. The video corroborated Tom's statement that there had been a wire boobytrap and that someone had attacked him. But the brief frames showing the assailant wearing a balaclava would be of little help in identifying a suspect. Liu would share the video with forensics, but he didn't hold out much hope of learning anything from it. And having been attacked from behind, Tom had no other details to add.

"We're not getting a lot of breaks, are we?" Tom commented.

Liu had to agree but vowed to keep working to get to the truth.

Chapter 32:

PATRICK AND MIRIAM—*DAY 14*—AUGUST 27

*M*iriam and Tom's house—well, just Miriam's house now—is stunning, Patrick thought, as he pulled his black BMW into the drive.

With its Victorian styling and thick shrubbery lining the stone walkway to the front door, the house had a classic feel, as did most houses in this upscale area.

Patrick had driven along Summerhill's winding streets to this house for lots of casual one-on-one visits with Tom as well as elaborate parties that Miriam had staged for friends and clients. But today it felt very different being here, he realized as he rang the bell.

"Patrick, thanks so much for coming over," Miriam said. She wore a tailored soft gray jumpsuit that fit her to a T and showed off her petite figure.

"Do you want a coffee or maybe something a little stronger? It's after three, so it's not too early for happy hour," Miriam said, smiling.

Patrick suggested opening a bottle of red, and Miriam obliged with one of Tom's finer selections. They headed into what Miriam liked to call the conservatory—*a sunroom to most people*, Patrick thought.

It was a sumptuous but comfortable room with floor-to-ceiling windows that showcased the beautiful patio beyond. Neither Tom nor Miriam were gardeners, nor did they have time for home duties, so they had a maintenance company that managed the flowerbeds in summer and cleared snow in winter.

When Miriam and Patrick were seated in large wicker chairs with the sun streaming in, Patrick raised his glass. "Here's to you, Miriam. Despite everything you've been through, you look amazing," he said.

Miriam raised her glass in thanks. "You're sweet, Patrick, but I'm sure I look a mess. It hasn't been easy. . ." she said.

"I know, and I'm glad to be here for you," Patrick responded.

Patrick wasn't stupid. He recognized a cash cow situation when he saw one. Miriam's net worth had just skyrocketed, with real estate and investment assets worth millions that were now in her sole possession. Meanwhile, Patrick had been ousted just in time for what he suspected was the next big step for Pellucid. He had heard rumors about acquisitions and IPOs before he was fired.

If those fools thought they would exclude me from my rightful piece of that, they were mistaken! Patrick thought.

However, given the clause in his employment agreement that fixed the total amount he could receive upon exit, winning over Miriam would be a convenient way to regain his status.

So let the charm offensive begin, he mused.

After all, Miriam was an attractive woman. She might not be his type, but a man could make accommodations for special circumstances. She could be his conduit back into good standing at Pellucid. And he truly did feel sorry for Miriam that more and more, she had felt like second best compared to Elise from Tom's perspective.

"I find myself wondering if I should keep such a big house with just me rattling around in it. I'm nervous on my own here at night despite having a good security system. But hopefully, I'll get past that," Miriam said.

"I'm sure it will get easier over time," Patrick said.

He was thinking that not having her usual schedule at the art gallery probably wasn't helping. Miriam had told him she hadn't gone back to work yet because there was so much paperwork to prepare and file. She was getting everything ready so that when the coroner finally released Tom's death certificate, she would be done with government forms.

"Well, at least on top of everything else, I trust you won't have financial worries," Patrick said.

"Yes, I'm fortunate that finances aren't a concern. I did take out a personal life insurance policy on Tom last summer. Do you remember when we talked about that at the company party at Lawrence's cottage?"

"I remember it well. And I haven't forgotten our time alone at the boathouse," Patrick said, remembering kissing Miriam passionately while music from the Pellucid party echoed down from the cottage.

Miriam looked a little flustered.

"That shouldn't have happened, and it was my fault, I'm sure. Too much wine out in the sun," she said, blushing.

That's only part of it, Patrick thought. It had been clear to him that Miriam found him attractive and no doubt she had appreciated his interest in the absence of Tom's attention.

"I'm glad it happened, but that's just me," Patrick said, smiling and then moving on. "So, you did decide to take out a policy?"

"Yes, half a million life insurance coverage with double indemnity in case of accident. As I was telling you that day, I felt a bit exposed because what if Tom made different choices in life, and we weren't married anymore? If that happened before Pellucid made it big, there would be a huge amount of wealth that wouldn't be joint property," Miriam said.

"I told Tom I just wanted to be less dependent on him and have something in my name, and Tom said he understood and he signed the insurance documents. But the truth is that I felt I needed to protect myself financially," Miriam added.

"That was smart thinking, Miriam," Patrick said, hoping his delight at the news wasn't super obvious. "Considering what happened to Tom, you never know what's coming next in life."

Miriam nodded and refilled their glasses. As she moved closer to him with the wine, Patrick could detect the light, breezy fragrance that was Miriam's trademark scent. *Miriam is quickly becoming even more attractive*, he thought, lightly touching her arm as he thanked her for the wine.

"You sounded upset about the reading of the will," Patrick said.

"I was—and I still am. The thing that didn't sit well with me was the provision for Titan, and by Titan I mean Elise. Tom left an obscene amount of money for her and that horse!" Miriam said. "I freely admit it was difficult to have Tom so enamored with Elise, and this was kind of a final insult."

"Not to mention that Elise and Winston are now co-CEOs—at least until the board decides on permanent leadership," Patrick said.

"Yes, that's ridiculous in my opinion. She's only in charge of marketing, after all!" Miriam said.

"Well, at this point, Tom and Elise are no longer an issue, so it's probably best if you try to let go of that," Patrick said gently. "But where Pellucid is headed at this point is something that you may want to weigh in on."

"I'll do my best to get past the whole Elise thing, but it's hard. As for Pellucid, as you know I've been a board member pretty much in name only. But I would like to be more involved now, especially in deciding who will take Tom's place as CEO. It certainly won't be Elise if I have any say," Miriam said firmly.

Miriam excused herself to make up a plate of cheese, crackers, and prosciutto to enjoy with their wine. When she returned to the room and set the plate on the coffee table, she stopped and put her delicate hand on Patrick's solid shoulder.

"I'm glad you're here, Patrick. It's comforting to be able to talk about these things with someone I trust," she said, as she returned to her chair.

"Anytime," Patrick said. "You know, I was thinking that you might be entitled to more shares and have more sway in your own right than what it appears at the moment. I've worked with a good corporate lawyer who could advise on that, given Pellucid's growth during your marriage to Tom," Patrick said.

"Wow, that never even occurred to me," said Miriam. "I'd like to have the lawyer's take on it."

"I've also been hearing rumors of an acquisition offer?" Patrick said.

"Yes, but my father and I aren't on board with selling the company at this stage. He thinks Pellucid has a lot more potential in its own right. He wants to help lead that going forward," Miriam said.

"Maybe we could support him by lobbying some of the board members who are leaning toward selling the company," Patrick said.

"I'm sure my father would be pleased to have our help," Miriam said enthusiastically. "We'll have to act fast though, because the board meeting is coming up in two weeks."

"Okay, I'll contact the lawyer and get his input on the share allocations," Patrick said. "And then maybe we can speak with James regarding the board."

"Perfect," Miriam said. "You know, this is the first time I've felt remotely happy about anything since all this happened."

"I'm glad to hear that," Patrick said, and then paused. "Miriam, can I ask you something else?"

"You can always ask, but you may not always get an answer," Miriam said coyly, laughing.

"Do you have any reason to think that Tom's death was anything but an accident?" Patrick asked.

"You mean foul play?"

"Yes, that's what I'm wondering," Patrick said.

"What a peculiar thought. No. How could it be? What made you think of that?" Miriam said.

"Oh, just something Elise mentioned in passing. I'm sure it's nothing, just her imagination working overtime."

"And there she is, causing trouble for no reason!" Miriam said, annoyed with Elise again. "I wouldn't give that ridiculous idea another thought."

As the sun started to fade, Patrick decided he'd accomplished enough for one day and would head home. When he and Miriam stood in the foyer saying goodbye, he gave her a warm hug and a kiss on the cheek and felt her relax in his arms.

Driving away from the elegant neighborhood, he realized he couldn't lose, no matter what happened.

Plan A: he gets back into Pellucid through Miriam because she gains more control, sidelining Elise and Winston. Plan B: he just gets in well with Miriam and all that wonderful money.

Isn't it nice when a plan comes together? Patrick congratulated himself.

 *Chapter 33:*

ELISE—*DAY 14*—AUGUST 27

The fiasco at the barn with Patrick the day before had been enough to convince Elise that sharing the contents of the video with anyone but the police would be a mistake. There was a killer at large, and it was time to make the authorities aware and let professionals investigate, Elise concluded.

She surmised that since the incident happened in Caledon, she would probably need to connect with the Orangeville OPP who serve that area.

Before leaving for the office, Elise summoned the courage to call and was connected with an OPP officer who seemed familiar with the situation. He took her contact information and noted her concerns, advising that someone would be back in touch.

Elise wasn't convinced anyone was going to take this seriously based on a single video, but all she could do was wait.

 *Chapter 34:*

DETECTIVE LIU—*DAY 14*—AUGUST 27

etective Liu had indeed attended Tom's memorial service to surreptitiously see if anything seemed unusual, or if someone had shown up who looked out of place. And he had kept tabs on what had happened next, including the reading of the will at the Pellucid office.

Liu had also filled Tom in on what was going on beyond the confines of the safe house, and Tom said it felt like someone had walked on his grave. Liu could only imagine what it would be like knowing that people had honored you with a memorial service and read the contents of your will while you were still alive. *It probably feels like something out of a Stephen King novel*, Liu thought.

But despite staying on top of things, Liu was completely taken aback when Orangeville OPP called him at the office that morning to report that Elise Armstrong was asserting Tom's death wasn't an accident based on a video she had discovered.

Liu immediately called Tom to ask how Elise would know the contents of the video from the day of the attack.

"Oh, damn, I completely forgot that when they had the reading of the will, my lawyer would have given Elise a key to my safe deposit box with passwords to my video files," Tom responded. "She must have accessed the cloud storage file from that day."

"That makes sense," Liu said. "But it adds a layer of complexity because now someone aside from yourself and the perp knows that this was a deliberate attack. I need to ensure that Elise doesn't share this with anyone, because that could put her at risk."

Tom agreed, and Detective Liu immediately called Elise, explained that he was following up on her call to the Orangeville OPP, and arranged to meet at her King Street West condo that evening.

 *Chapter 35:*

LIU AND ELISE—*DAY 14*—AUGUST 27

The tall, slim woman who greeted him this Friday night was strikingly attractive despite wearing little makeup and being casually dressed in jeans and a T-shirt. Elise invited him in, and Liu noted that the condo was spacious and tastefully decorated with a modern, uncluttered but homey feel. He and Elise sat down at her dining table where she already had her laptop open.

"So let me first say how sorry I am for the loss of Tom Oliver. I'm sure that has been very hard for everyone at Pellucid, Ms. Armstrong," Detective Liu said.

"Thank you. It *has* been tough," Elise said, swallowing and looking away. "And please just call me Elise."

"Okay, Elise, let's start with some background for me, if you don't mind," Liu said. "Tell me about your history with Pellucid and what's going on there at the moment."

She described how she had joined the company four years prior and had collaborated with Tom to build the Pellucid brand. Elise noted the prospects for the company and the current controversy over acquisition. Liu then moved quickly to the matter at hand.

"Did Tom happen to share anything with you about concerns for his own safety before he died?"

Elise looked shocked. "No, and he usually tells me—told me—anything important like that."

"A couple of weeks before the tragedy, Tom had a near miss with a vehicle that veered onto the sidewalk and almost hit him. That happened after a dinner meeting in Yorkville," Liu shared.

"Oh, my God, that's awful. I can't imagine why he didn't say something," Elise said. "How do you know about this?"

"I was on duty when Tom came into police headquarters to report the incident. He probably didn't want to worry you unnecessarily. And he wasn't convinced someone wanted to harm him, although he did have some suspicions that he was being followed recently," Liu said.

"Oh, my God," Elise repeated.

"That's why I'm looking into your report, because this is already an open investigation," Liu explained. "Elise, do you know of anyone who would want to kill Tom?"

"No, no one. He was one of the best people I've ever known," Elise said, biting her lower lip to keep her emotions under control.

"What about Patrick McGowan? I hear he was pretty angry at being fired."

By Elise's expression, Liu could see she was surprised that he already knew about Patrick's departure from Pellucid.

"Yes, he was, but Patrick and Tom were friends for more than five years before that happened. And Patrick is hot-tempered, but he could never be a murderer," Elise said.

"In my experience, there are a lot of people you'd think couldn't commit murder, and then, boom!" Liu said, making Elise jump when he illustrated "boom!" by whacking his hand on the table. "Oh, sorry about that!"

"That's fine," Elise said, managing a smile. "Um, Tom's brother, Nate, is the only other person who caused Tom a lot of angst, and they did have a heated exchange when Nate came to the office on Tom's last day at work."

Liu nodded and made note of that.

"Good to know. Let's talk about the video you mentioned. How did you come to find that footage?"

Elise explained how she had been given the key by the lawyer and then checked the video files.

"Let's have a look," Liu said.

Elise used AirPlay to share the video on the TV so they could watch the footage together in a larger format. Liu looked keen and pretended it was the first time he had seen it. He asked her to play it a second time.

"Well, you were certainly right to bring this to my attention, Elise, and it does indicate foul play," Detective Liu said. "Do you mind if I copy that onto a USB stick to take to my forensics guys?"

"No problem," Elise said, quickly copying the video file.

"Since finding this, have you mentioned anything to anyone about the possibility of murder?" Liu asked.

"Not in so many words," Elise said. "But yesterday, I ran into Patrick McGowan at the stable in Caledon—the one where Tom's horse is boarded, and Patrick and I both ride too."

Liu's eyebrows raised slightly, but he didn't comment, just kept making notes.

"When Patrick pressed me about why I was at the stable on a workday, I alluded to the fact that I wanted to see for myself where Tom died and whether it made sense an accident could happen there," Elise said.

Liu was surprised that Elise would check out the scene on her own. Brave woman.

"How did Patrick react to your comment?"

"He accused me of not being able to move on from Tom's death. And he thought foul play was a crazy idea," Elise said.

"But he doesn't know about the video, right?"

"No, I haven't mentioned it to anyone," she said.

"That's good, Elise. Until we get a handle on what looks like murder based on this video, it's important that you don't tell anyone else anything at all about this. And if you see Patrick again, tell him that he was right—you got carried away because you were having a bad day and you've dropped the notion of foul play. I'm not trying to scare you, but someone attacked Tom, and you can't trust anyone," Liu cautioned.

"Of course, I understand. It was a bad move to share anything with Patrick," Elise said, looking distressed.

"You were taken by surprise by him being at the barn. I get that," Liu said kindly. "Just be extra careful while we investigate. Don't stay late at the office by yourself and avoid walking at night on your own. Play it safe until we know more."

Elise nodded.

"By the way, did you find anything important at the scene?" Liu asked, not letting on that the location had already been scoured by police.

"It had rained heavily, so there wasn't much to find. The trees where the wire was attached had some bark scraped off, and someone may have cleared a path to the adjacent side road. Not much really," Elise said.

"Okay, we'll check it out," Liu said. "And thanks for your time. Feel free to call me anytime if you have any concerns. If I don't pick up, my office will reach me for you. And if you think of anything, even the smallest detail that could help us, let me know."

"I will for sure," Elise agreed.

Liu stood up to leave and handed Elise his card.

"And don't do any more sleuthing without me," Liu said with a smile.

"I promise!" Elise confirmed.

As he left, he knew Elise would be struggling to think of who could have done this horrible thing and why. She was probably also coming to terms with the fact that she could be in danger. And Liu couldn't help feeling guilty that Elise was suffering, believing that Tom was dead.

 *Chapter 36:*

DETECTIVE LIU—*DAY 14*—AUGUST 27

When Liu left Elise's place he headed to his favorite Friday night venue, the outdoor patio at Bar Wellington. He needed a break and ordered a beer, watching as people passed by while music wafted out of the main restaurant.

After busy workdays, Liu enjoyed being an anonymous observer rather than a participant in things unfolding around him. He had to admit that made him a bit of a lone wolf, having never married and barely making time even to socialize.

He suspected that was a big disappointment to his parents, since they wanted grandchildren for some reason that escaped him. Having adapted quickly to his new life in Canada, Liu thought that sometimes his parents' Canadianized son must seem quite different from their more traditional Chinese ways.

Their move to Canada had been part of the major migration wave that was fueled by the Tiananmen Square protests of 1989. His parents, both professionals, feared mainland Chinese repression in Hong Kong. So they had started over in Canada, opening an accounting firm that served a largely Asian clientele, although they lived in the Anglo-oriented neighborhood of Roncesvalles.

Having a smaller build than most of the boys from Polish and other European backgrounds who lived in the area, Liu decided to prove his worth by trying out for the high school football team and made the cut. What he lacked in size he made up for in smarts, speed, and surprising strength, so he proved to be a great running back.

Liu recalled meeting Tom and thinking he was a typical high school football jock, a born leader as the quarterback, and a strategic, determined player. When Liu got picked on by the other guys who called him Kung Fu instead of Liu, Tom would quickly shut that down.

Liu told Tom he could fight his own battles, but Tom didn't stop running interference. So one Friday after a game, Liu called him out on it and gave Tom a strong shove. The two of them got into it, but it wasn't a long skirmish because Liu put Tom in a wrist lock and threw him to the ground, knocking the wind out of him.

Tom had gasped for a while on his back in the grass trying to inhale. And then he started to chuckle because he had under-estimated Liu. They both ended up laughing so hard they couldn't speak, realizing how silly the whole thing had been.

"So, I guess I won't worry about you from now on," Tom had said, holding his ribs and taking Liu's outstretched hand to get back on his feet.

After that, they became close friends, and Liu was often the third boy at the Oliver dinner table. Tom and his family called him Jason, as did his own family, but outside that inner circle, Jason preferred to be called Liu.

Liu went into policing largely because of his exposure to Tom's father, with whom he formed a close bond. Chief Oliver had realized that neither of his sons was destined for policing, and he was thrilled to have a protégé in Jason. Nate in particular was relieved that Jason was filling the gap so his dad would quit pestering him about the virtues of being a police officer.

Liu felt as if he had lost his extended family when Tom's parents died. And he worried what would become of Nate, who was already less secure than Tom. Liu did his best to look out for Nate when Tom moved to England, but soon Nate was running with a different crowd, and not a good one.

When Tom and Miriam got married, Liu was one of his groomsmen at their wedding in Raleigh. Since then, with both so busy with their careers, he and Tom got together only a couple of times a year. But when they did, they always picked up seamlessly where they had left off. Liu knew Tom was a friend for life.

Liu had never mentioned to anyone at the police force that he had a connection to police royalty as it were, given the late Chief Oliver's star status. Liu didn't want preferential treatment. But when Tom was attacked, he certainly had extra motivation—and support—to see the investigation through to its conclusion.

As he sipped his second beer of the night, Liu thought about the challenges ahead and realized it would take a lot of effort to solve this case.

It's my turn to have Tom's back, and I won't let him down, Liu promised himself.

 *Chapter 37:*

NATE—*DAY 17*—AUGUST 30

Nate had scarcely been out of bed at his basement apartment since the reading of the will two days before. He checked his phone and found eight voicemails from his boss, the last one threatening to fire him if he didn't get in touch immediately. Not that a job at a call center was anything to be thrilled about, but it paid the bills.

What had fueled Nate's latest drinking binge was his brother's final gesture of over-management with the trust fund. Meting out payments and handcuffing him from what: extorting more money from others? It was plain for all to see that Tom had an incredibly low opinion of him. So Nate had no feelings of grief or guilt over Tom's death. Instead, he was furious. He had meant what he said when he told Tom he would be better off with him dead.

The bottle from the night before rolled onto the floor when Nate pulled back the comforter to get up and make a vodka and orange juice.

Breakfast of champions, he joked to himself. *Oh damn, there's that stray cat peering in the window above the kitchen sink again.*

The cat had been coming by off and on lately, and every time it left, Nate figured it wouldn't be back.

After all, I'm not exactly a reliable caregiver, Nate thought as he opened the ground-level window and lifted the cat down.

He gave the skinny gray cat some leftover tuna, which it ate greedily.

"You're just like me, eh?" Nate said. "Eating out of someone else's hand. Just don't bite the hand that feeds you like I did."

Nate had to admit to himself that he was what people call a functioning alcoholic, drinking outside work hours on weekdays and binging on weekends. It was getting harder on his system, so he was sick a lot. He knew if he didn't hit the brakes soon, he could wind up dead just like Tom. But he relied on numbing his feelings with as much alcohol as it took to make it through any given day.

Nate was aware that he was not a fun-loving, jovial drunk. Instead, drinking made him bold, and as a result, he had been in his share of bar fights. Many times, he had vented his frustration and anger by putting a fist through the drywall of the apartment, to the point the place was starting to look like a patchwork quilt of plaster repairs.

One of his biggest problems was not knowing what he wanted. Tom had always been so focused. "Goal-oriented," their dad called Tom. Their parents encouraged Tom's sports and especially his riding, since he was a brave cross-country competitor, and people always offered him their horses to ride and show.

It seemed like the bigger the shadow Tom cast with his achievements, the smaller corner was left for Nate to occupy. His parents had tried to be supportive of Nate's introspective interest in art and video gaming. While they admired the quality of the artwork, they couldn't relate to the subject matter that included detailed pencil sketches of people cowering in prison cells, tormented faces, and evil surreal characters. Like his feelings, Nate started to keep his artwork hidden and released his resentment playing violent games like *Call of Duty* in which he could obliterate everybody.

Nate had been keen on pursuing his art and thought Miriam's gallery might be an option when she started curating artwork in Yorkville. *Forget that*, Nate thought, as he remembered with annoyance how condescending Miriam was when he had taken some samples to show her.

"This doesn't really fit with my clients' sensibilities," she had said, and Nate had felt like reaching over and smacking her perfectly made-up, smug little face.

Well, now his brother was gone. No more shadow covering him. No more expectations. No one to be compared unfavorably to. No more having to ask for handouts. No more humiliation from Tom or Miriam. He would be master of his own domain with a trust fund giving him a regular paycheck.

Maybe this could be his time to come into the light and shine. He pushed the drink away and turned on the coffeepot. Then he called his boss and announced he was quitting his job.

It feels good to tell that overbearing jerk to shove his job where the sun doesn't shine! Nate thought indignantly.

When he opened the window again to let the cat back out, he welcomed the gust of fresh air that blew into the apartment.

 *Chapter 38:*

PATRICK, MIRIAM, AND JAMES—*DAY 18*— AUGUST 31

Patrick and Miriam sat on barstools at her massive kitchen island with her laptop open and coffee mugs in hand. They were waiting for her father to join their Zoom call to discuss the upcoming board meeting.

Patrick shared with Miriam that consulting his corporate lawyer contact had proven fruitful. Although there were no guarantees, a case could be made to the board that Miriam had been unfairly excluded from a rightful share of Tom's stock holdings that had been accumulated within Pellucid during the course of Tom and Miriam's marriage. If they could address the shareholdings at the outset of the board meeting, Miriam might have more sway over the issue of who would take over as CEO.

James logged in and greeted them from his office in Raleigh.

"Hi, darling—and I don't mean you, Patrick!" James joked.

"Hi, Daddy," Miriam responded with a laugh.

"Patrick, how are you?"

"I'm well, sir. How are things in North Carolina?" Patrick asked.

"Good, thanks. Lots going on though, so let's get to this board meeting business," James said. "I've read the materials you sent me on share allocation and that's positive. And I agree we should have the chairman—who is now Winston according to the shareholders' agreement—put that on the top of the agenda for the meeting. We also need to have a viable proposal for Tom's replacement as CEO."

"Daddy, I'm dead set against having Elise step in as CEO, as you know. That's my main concern here. And Patrick isn't keen on Winston, given he was party to his firing," Miriam said.

"Yes, and let me say that was unfortunate, Patrick," James said, and Patrick nodded his appreciation.

"I do have some news for you two that I think you'll like on the CEO front," James continued. "I've spoken with a colleague, George Carson, who leads Google's digital innovation team, and he's ready to make his next move. His wife just got a transfer to Toronto, so he's open to opportunities there. I'd like to propose new blood for Pellucid under someone who has the leadership acumen to take Pellucid a long way, and George is the perfect candidate."

Patrick and Miriam looked at each other with some surprise at the suggestion of an outside hire.

"That's intriguing, James," Patrick said. "Having a clean slate could move the company forward. And it wouldn't hurt me either, if I come back to Pellucid at some point," Patrick said, smiling.

"I hope you do, Patrick, as I'm thinking you could be a good business development leader for us again," James said.

"Thank you, sir," Patrick said, while thinking perhaps James wasn't fully in the loop as to the details of his firing, or he might not be so supportive.

"Just out of interest, how do you know George?" Patrick asked.

"We worked together about ten years ago before I started my company, and I was always impressed with his work ethic and leadership style," James said. "And George is a real go-getter, so he's not going to want to divest Pellucid right away. He'll want to make his mark, build the business, and maybe even go for an IPO in the future. I don't favor acquisition at this point, so that's another benefit of bringing George on board."

"Well, it seems like a great option. Miriam, what are your thoughts?" Patrick asked.

Miriam was unaccustomed to being asked for her opinion on such things, and Patrick could tell that being asked made her feel even more appreciated by him.

"It all sounds good to me. It's time for a change, and an outside candidate could be the answer, especially since he has my father's endorsement," she replied.

"Since we're all in agreement, I'll send an email to Winston asking for a review of share allocations to be added to the top of the agenda. I'm sure the CEO selection is already an agenda item, but I'll confirm it when I speak to him," said James.

"Perfect, thanks, James," Patrick said.

"Bye, Daddy," Miriam closed off.

Patrick and Miriam instantaneously picked up their mugs, clinked them together, and said, "Cheers!"—excited about the progress made to gain control of Pellucid. And Miriam said how delighted she was at how things were coming together.

As he headed home, Patrick turned and gave Miriam a big hug, lifting her off the floor and adding an intense kiss to seal the deal, seeming to leave her breathless.

"Patrick, why don't you come back for dinner tonight," Miriam suggested.

As Patrick accepted, he thought from the look in her eyes he would be staying for more than just dinner.

 *Chapter 39:*

LAWRENCE, WINSTON, AND ELISE—*DAY 19*— SEPTEMBER 1

I t sounded important when Winston called him, so Lawrence had made time in his schedule almost immediately to meet with Winston and Elise at the Pellucid office. The next board meeting was coming up and would be a big one in deciding the company's fate. With his end goal of having the acquisition completed, Lawrence was keen to hear the latest on what had been happening behind the scenes.

Elise and Winston greeted him warmly when he arrived.

"Lawrence, so good to see you," Winston said, indicating he should make himself comfortable.

"Good to see you both as well," Lawrence responded.

Lawrence noticed that Elise looked model-thin, which was not necessarily a healthy thing, and Winston looked tired.

"So fill me in on the latest. I feel out of touch," Lawrence said, as he lowered his large frame onto the leather sofa in Winston's office.

Winston explained that he had heard from a couple of board members about agenda items. Of course, the lineup for the meeting included Winston providing an update on the status of the acquisition offer. And with Tom's passing, his replacement as CEO was up for discussion.

"I called you because I thought you should know that James has a particular interest in the CEO selection, and he wants to ensure that's a priority on the agenda. And he also wants to table discussion on allocation of shares, presumably something to do with Miriam," Winston said.

"Hmmm, that's interesting," Lawrence mused. "Knowing James, he has something up his sleeve regarding control of the company and especially the CEO position. We need to have our ducks in a row.

"Elise, if the board were to put you forward for the position, would you want to take on the CEO post?" Lawrence asked.

"No," Elise responded without hesitation. "I enjoy providing counsel to the CEO and sharing in decision-making where my input is valued, but my strength is in building the brand. The best spot for me to put Pellucid on the map is in my current role as chief marketing officer. So no, accepting a nomination for CEO would not be in Pellucid's best interests."

"That's a thoughtful answer and an unselfish one. Winston, what are your thoughts on becoming CEO?" Lawrence asked.

"As CFO I've had the opportunity to understand the inner workings of the company and gain insight as to where Tom was taking the business," Winston said. "With an appreciation for the big shoes Tom left to fill, I would accept a nomination if the board asked me to step into the CEO role."

"So there we have it. Elise, are you comfortable with an endorsement for Winston as CEO?"

"Absolutely," Elise said with a smile in Winston's direction.

"I am as well, Winston, so I'll plan to nominate you when the CEO question arises at the meeting," Lawrence said.

"As to the matter of the acquisition, it's my understanding that you favor selling the company over continuing to develop

Pellucid independently. Do I have that right, Winston?" Lawrence asked.

"Yes, I'm all for keeping this acquisition offer from Crystal Clere viable," Winston replied.

"Elise, I know you don't typically have a vote since you're not on the board of directors. But as interim co-CEO you will have voting rights this time around. If you don't mind sharing with us, have you made a decision on that?" Lawrence asked.

"Yes. If Crystal Clere is still willing to move forward, I think we should accept," Elise said. "It's a great opportunity to monetize the value of what Tom founded and created."

"I agree, Elise! So, the three of us are in agreement on accepting Crystal Clere's offer. But James does not support the acquisition and has been vocal about it. That means Miriam will join her father against the acquisition," Lawrence said. "But the position of several board members who aren't part of the Pellucid team is unknown at this point, so we need to start reaching out to them."

Winston grabbed a marker at the whiteboard and made a list of the board members. They then divided up what they considered the few "uncommitted" members for follow-up chats before the September 10 meeting.

"We also need to be cognizant that Tom had been expecting to receive Crystal Clere's letter of intent, but that letter hadn't been received before Tom died and we still haven't seen it. Crystal Clere could be reassessing the acquisition given the potential for Tom's passing to impact Pellucid's prospects," Lawrence said.

"That's right, Lawrence, and I'm concerned about that," Winston said. "We have to demonstrate stability, so I've been preparing a thirty-, sixty-, ninety-day plan for how we can continue to manage the business effectively and profitably, and how we can minimize the implications of losing our founder and CEO."

"I've also taken the step of identifying people to backfill me in the CFO position, should the board endorse me to be the next CEO," Winston added.

"That's excellent, Winston. Hopefully Pellucid can continue to achieve strong revenue growth so the offer—and the valuation Crystal Clere proposed—stays in play."

Their meeting concluded just in time for Lawrence to leave for a Global News interview: "The top ten stocks for bullish investors in fall 2021."

As Lawrence got into an Uber, he was thinking that the spotlight was now shining on Winston's ability to lead the company to a successful acquisition. And Lawrence vowed to himself that he would allocate whatever time was needed to help Winston and Elise make the deal a reality.

 *Chapter 40:*

DETECTIVE LIU—*DAY 19*—SEPTEMBER 1

Detective Liu was growing increasingly impatient with the investigation of Tom's case. A few bits and pieces of information had surfaced, but nothing definitive for a real break. And despite having the video footage, there were zero clues as to the identity of the attacker.

As he leaned back in his chair and ate his lunch at his desk, Liu studied the cast of characters mounted on his bulletin board. He must be missing something in the sphere of influence and contacts surrounding Tom.

Tom was at the center of the board, with connections emanating outward like concentric circles, characters involved in Tom's life in some way—personal, professional, or both. For the moment, it was a wide web, and overall, it was hard to picture Tom having an enemy with sufficient motivation for murder.

Tom is someone most people would want for a son, brother, friend, partner—loyal to a fault, savvy in business but not ruthless. So how could his connection to these people, or perhaps someone not yet known to police, have resulted in murder attempts? Liu wondered.

Liu's focus turned to Miriam's photo. Tom's wife had always struck Liu as a cold fish, but as police had observed from surveillance, it hadn't taken long for her to get cozy with Tom's former friend Patrick McGowan—a matter of days, not months, Liu noted. He suspected that particular liaison wasn't entirely new.

Investigation showed that Miriam had taken out a life insurance policy that summer for a hefty amount with double indemnity in case of accident.

She would make out like a bandit in the event of his death, Liu thought.

Liu had not ruled Miriam out of having some sort of involvement, although she certainly didn't have the physical capability to have attacked Tom herself.

McGowan, on the other hand, certainly had the strength to do it. Could he and Miriam have colluded to kill Tom, with Miriam gaining a lover and a pile of money, and McGowan potentially benefiting significantly through Miriam's wealth?

McGowan had been livid with Tom for being fired, holding him personally responsible, so motivations of resentment and greed made him a prime suspect. Liu had never met him, so he had no prior knowledge of the man. But from what Tom had told him, he sounded like someone with a quick temper.

Next on the bulletin board was Tom's brother, Nate, whom Liu knew to be a rather sullen and withdrawn personality. Nate had a record for drug possession from thirteen years prior and a few incidents within the last few years of being drunk in a public place, but otherwise he had stayed off the police radar.

Talk about polar opposites in the same family, Liu thought, with Tom being a high achiever and Nate always a disgrace to his father's memory. On a personal level, Liu had no use for Nate bringing shame to the Oliver family's good name.

The fact that Nate had been even angrier than usual with Tom the day before the attack was concerning. Tom had assured Liu that Nate could barely organize himself for a trip to the mall, let alone plan a murder. But stranger things have happened for money, so Liu was not sure whether Nate was still as incompetent as ever, or if he had made a plan that would get him out from under his brother's shadow. Nate knew full well that Tom wouldn't leave him high and dry if he died, and true to form, Tom's will had included a hefty trust fund allocation for Nate.

Another potential suspect was Winston Wilson, Pellucid CFO and now acting chairman and co-CEO. Tom and Winston were not social outside the office but had a close working relationship. Tom had assured Liu that Winston was a straight shooter, very low on his list of potential suspects. Nevertheless, Liu was watching for any unusual moves by Winston before the upcoming board meeting.

Is Winston keen enough to become CEO that he would murder Tom to get him out of the way? Stranger things have happened, Liu thought.

Liu had added finance influencer Lawrence Cameron to the suspect wall. Liu had done some digging with contacts at CTV News and heard rumors that the Big Guy, as he's known, was looking to amplify his US-related credentials to benefit his new role as a commentator on a major cable network in the States. *Seeing the acquisition completed would be pretty important to him*, Liu thought. But with his financial empire and an already impressive following, Lawrence was an unlikely candidate to be a murderer.

Lawrence and Tom got along well, with Lawrence serving as something of a mentor, and there was no apparent motivation for murder on the Big Guy's part. A background check showed Lawrence had no skeletons in the closet aside from a messy divorce from his first wife.

Also, on the wall but not a key player was Miriam's father, James Robinson. Liu had met Robinson at Tom's wedding, but nothing stood out in his memory about him other than his extreme pride walking his only child down the aisle. Robinson had been in North Carolina for the three months prior to Tom's memorial service with no travel to Canada, and as a board member at Pellucid, he would have nothing to gain from Tom's death.

Elise's photo was on the bulletin board, but Liu was confident that Elise had nothing to do with the attempts on Tom's life. Her dedication to Tom was obvious, and the fact she had brought the video to the attention of police confirmed she was not involved.

Liu had another spot on the bulletin board that contained a blank outline of a human figure. That icon represented all the other unforeseen possibilities that might not yet have come to light. *That's the unknown entity of which nightmares are made*, Liu thought.

As he and Tom had discussed back when the Yorkville incident happened, could the unknown attacker be someone from Tom's past who held a grudge for whatever reason?

Or could it be someone who had fared poorly during the pandemic and resented a successful and affluent CEO not only surviving but thriving? Liu wondered.

As Liu finished the last of his lunch, he faced the fact that the investigation was not much further along than when they had spirited Tom away to the safe house. Tom would be getting anxious to resume his life and reassure everyone that he was still alive. Liu recognized that the case was going to need a new strategy.

Chapter 41:

TOM AND LIU—*DAY 20*–SEPTEMBER 2

I t had been almost three weeks since the attack, and Tom was feeling much more himself now. The headaches had eased off, and if he took care to avoid straining his eyes, the flashes of light were much less frequent.

One advantage of being taken out of his ordinary life was that he had a forced quiet recovery period with no option of overdoing things. Dr. Anderson was pleased with his progress, and now instead of checkups, he had started coming over to play chess and even approved of Tom having a little Scotch the other night.

Liu had given approval for Tom to use his laptop but had cautioned against opening any sites where Tom's identity could be tracked or someone could notice him logging into an account. It was driving Tom crazy not to know the status of things at work, given the impending board meeting, but there would be no point to the whole safe house strategy if Tom inadvertently undermined things by coming out of the shadows.

Tom was keen to meet with Liu this afternoon to get an update and see if staging his death had been productive. Liu arrived at the door just as Tom was lining up his arguments for coming back to life.

"Fancy meeting you here," Liu joked as Tom made him a coffee in the small kitchen of the safe house.

"Ha, well, I have to tell you I'm getting pretty sick of seeing the same four walls, and it's a tough time not to be working with my team at Pellucid given what's going on with the business," Tom said.

"I hear you, and I agree that we need to take stock and decide where we go from here," Liu said.

"Great!" Tom said.

He listened intently as Liu mapped out his latest findings, some of which were not easy for Tom to hear.

Liu first addressed Miriam, the additional life insurance she had purchased that summer, and the fact that she and Patrick McGowan were now together a great deal.

Tom shared with Liu that when he had signed the insurance documents, he had thought the coverage to be excessive given his and Miriam's significant net worth. But he had signed because it seemed to make Miriam feel more independent.

As for Patrick having surfaced, Tom attributed Patrick's involvement with Miriam as the actions of a concerned friend looking out for her.

Liu had no recourse but to tell Tom police had seen Patrick's car parked at Miriam's house the past two nights.

"I'll spare you the photos from our investigator, but there's no question that Miriam and Patrick are together," Liu said.

Tom took a long pause and then said dryly, "That was quick. Less than three weeks. Must be some kind of rebound record."

"I'm sorry, Tom," Liu said, feeling bad for his friend.

Liu then brought Tom up-to-date on forensics that had netted very little. While he had some suspicions, there was still nothing definitive to go on.

"With you supposedly dead, it impedes the investigation somewhat. I can't bring people in for questioning, given no one is aware that this was an attempted murder," Liu said. "It could be helpful to get more information from inside Pellucid and your inner circle, Tom."

"So what's next then?" Tom asked.

"I'd like to involve Elise," Liu replied.

Chapter 42:

ELISE AND LIU—*DAY 21*—SEPTEMBER 3

Elise had been surprised to get a call the previous night from Detective Liu, asking if he could stop by her condo before she went to the office today. He didn't offer any explanation, just said that he needed to speak with her.

Elise hoped it was because there had been progress in the murder case. She was curious but, at the same time, afraid to find out. She had a coffee but couldn't face eating any breakfast until perhaps later, after Detective Liu had delivered whatever news he had to share.

When the detective arrived promptly at eight thirty, she ushered him into the living room. He declined an offer of coffee and sat down in the chair opposite hers, looking as anxious as Elise felt.

Whatever this is, it can't be good, Elise thought.

The detective stared at his notepad and shifted uncomfortably, and Elise wished he would get on with it. He finally looked at her intently and said words she never could have imagined.

"Elise, there's something I have to tell you, and it's going to come as a shock after what you've been through. Tom Oliver is not dead," Liu said.

"What? That's not possible! How can that be true?" Elise said, not believing what she was hearing.

"Tom is alive, and he's in a safe house not far from here," Liu responded.

"And he's alright? What about the attack? Was he badly hurt?" Elise asked.

"Tom was a very lucky man. It could have been much worse. He had lacerations on his neck and some concussion symptoms, but overall he's been recovering well," Liu said.

"I can't believe you kept this from me! The last time you were here—you knew?" Elise said incredulously.

"Yes, but we couldn't jeopardize Tom's safety by telling anyone," Liu said.

"This is crazy! My God, I don't know what to feel first," Elise said. "I can't believe it—but, I mean if it's true, this is such good news! It's still so awful that someone would want to hurt Tom like that. And it's so sad he had to recover in a strange house all alone. But I'm so thankful he's still alive!"

Elise's mind was spinning as she tried to absorb what she had just heard. She barely noticed when the detective went to the kitchen and poured a glass of water for her.

"I wish I could have known he was still alive—and staying close to my place!" Elise said, accepting the glass from Liu.

"Tom wanted to tell you, but we wouldn't let him in case it jeopardized your safety," Liu responded.

Elise took that information in for a moment.

"Well, you have no idea just how awful it's been since that day," Elise said, tears welling up in her eyes. "It's a horrible thing to go through, believing someone you care about is dead and—worse than that—murdered!"

Elise stood up and turned her back to Liu, staring out the window while feeling complete shock, anger, and confusion.

"I understand how distressing this must be, and I can only apologize for the deception. But Tom's well-being was and continues to be our main concern," Liu said. "We couldn't risk another attack on his life that could result in his death. The safe house was a necessary step."

"I get that, but it's just been hard," Elise said. "Why did you decide it was okay for me to know now? Does anyone else know Tom's alive?" Elise asked.

"No one except law enforcement and the medical team knows," Liu said.

"Not even Miriam?" Elise asked, amazed.

Liu shook his head to indicate 'no' in a way that made Elise wonder if there was more to the story of not telling Miriam.

"To be honest, Elise, we're not making much progress on the case. There's just not a lot to go on. I'd like your help to get a handle on what's going on within Pellucid and your insights on Tom's inner circle, anything you might notice that's unusual. Maybe something will come to light that could move the case forward."

"I'm not sure what I can contribute, but of course I'll help," Elise said.

"There's something else you should know," Liu said.

Elise's eyebrows raised as she wondered what else could possibly be coming.

"I've known Tom since we were teenagers, and that's why he came to me when the Yorkville incident happened. So, I can assure you that I'm fully committed to finding whoever has been trying to kill him," Liu said.

"That's good to know," Elise said. "In the meantime, will I be able to see Tom or at least talk to him, or does he have to stay isolated?" Elise asked.

"I can arrange to take you to see Tom," Liu said. "When you're ready."

 *Chapter 43:*

LIU, TOM, AND ELISE—*DAY 21*—SEPTEMBER 3

Elise had asked Liu to leave so she could gather her thoughts and said she would connect with him later that day if she felt up to seeing Tom. Liu was relieved when she called a few hours later to say she wanted to see Tom as soon as possible.

After picking Elise up at the condo, Liu deliberately drove his sedan in the wrong direction and through a labyrinth of side streets before circling back to the location of the safe house. Liu was always cognizant that someone could be watching, and it paid to take precautions.

They entered the house, and Liu called out for Tom. Elise looked shocked when Tom came out of the kitchen, large as life.

"Ellie!" Tom exclaimed, smiling.

She ran to him and threw her arms around his neck. "Tom, I really thought you were dead! I can't believe you're here," Elise said, and she started to sob while touching his face to reassure herself that he was real.

"I'm so sorry! I hated having to put you through all this," he said, holding her close for a long hug.

Liu quickly excused himself and said he would be back later to talk strategy. For now, these two needed to get caught up.

Tom could see that Elise had lost weight, and she was much frailer than usual. This facade had taken a toll, and he was disappointed that, so far, it had all been for nothing. Tom flinched when she had put her arms around his neck, and it obviously made Elise sad to see the fresh scars from his wounds.

When the initial emotion had eased off and Elise had regained her composure, they poured some much-needed wine and sat on the couch in the living room. The house was small and sparingly furnished, but the original bay window looking out to the street let in lots of natural light. This September midafternoon was lovely and sunny, and they sat close together, not wanting to be separated after such a terrible absence.

Tom wanted to know everything that had been going on, starting with his horse. Elise told him about Titan and the slash to his shoulder, and Tom was distressed to know that Titan had been injured. In fact, he was even angrier that someone had hurt his horse than he was about being attacked himself. He was grateful to Elise for caring for Titan and spending time with him. And he wanted to hear all about the prep work underway at Pellucid.

Finally, he asked if Elise was aware of Miriam and Patrick's liaison.

Elise conceded that she had heard that Patrick and Miriam were together. She hadn't been surprised, given a coworker had seen Patrick and Miriam kissing at Lawrence's cottage that summer. Although Tom hadn't been aware of the summertime dalliance, he shared with Elise that things had not been ideal between him and Miriam for some time. Elise also told Tom about encountering Patrick at the barn and that he still seemed resentful about everything.

It was disappointing for Tom to hear about Miriam and Patrick being intimate earlier in the summer. Now, though, he couldn't blame her for moving on with Patrick because, after all, he was supposedly dead. But the speed with which his wife had moved on was hard to fathom.

When Elise mentioned the memorial service, Tom joked that he had sadly missed a good party. He was immediately sorry for making light of things because Elise cried again, no doubt thinking of the horrible sense of loss she'd felt that day. All Tom could do was put his arm around her and console her. He was grateful that he was still alive and that Elise was in his life.

"Ellie, can you ever forgive me for this whole charade? I swear I didn't want you to have to go through this," Tom said, hopeful that things could be the same as always between them.

"Of course," Elise responded. "It's not your fault, and I'd rather this than have someone come after you again!"

Tom gave a huge sigh of relief. "Thank you," he said, squeezing her hand. "That means so much to me."

———

As promised, Liu returned within a couple of hours, and Tom and Elise seemed much more settled after having a chance to talk things through. Now it was time to lay out the new strategy.

First Liu defined the ground rules of Elise knowing of Tom's existence.

Elise would need to give an Academy Award–winning performance to conceal the relief she was feeling about Tom's reappearance. No one else could know that he was still alive, Liu emphasized. She could not visit him at the safe house, since her coming and going could blow the cover. They were to use the burner cells he provided to communicate, never their own phones.

The purpose of Elise's involvement would be to note anything unusual happening at the office, any transactional activity she might see, or other strategic moves by key players. Elise would be Liu's eyes and ears inside the company, and she would serve as Tom's conduit to Pellucid since he still couldn't access any Pellucid files or information without disclosing his existence. Tom would remain in the safe house during the ongoing investigation.

When their planning was complete, Liu dropped Elise back at her condo. Elise shared with him that she felt emotionally wrung out but ecstatic and he was glad she now knew the truth about Tom. He suspected that Tom and Elise would be chatting more on their burner phones that night, making up for lost time.

 *Chapter 44:*

JAMES IN NORTH CAROLINA—*DAY 22—*
SEPTEMBER 4

I t had been a busy time for James between his company, the church, and the important work he was doing for the Republican Party. And through it all, he was trying to be supportive of his daughter, Miriam, who needed him now more than ever.

Miriam had held up well at the memorial service, but James wondered if the full realization of Tom's death had truly hit her. There are supposedly five stages of grief, and Miriam seemed to be stuck in one of them—anger—rather than sorrow for the loss of her husband.

However, that's just fine if she can move forward without ever experiencing the depth of pain I dealt with when her mother died, James reflected.

James had never remarried after his wife's passing. It was a combination of being busy building his business and being cognizant of needing just the right life partner to be an asset to his political career. For the last couple of years, he had been seeing a woman who attended his church, and a casual dating situation suited him fine for now.

He firmly disagreed with divorce and took the "till death do us part" promise seriously, so it was important to make the right personal decisions.

That was why he was concerned that things hadn't been ideal between Miriam and Tom for some time before Tom's death. Tom was not the choice he had envisioned for Miriam, and the disparity in values and background between the two of them had worried James from the get-go. Church and society were important to Miriam, and Tom had a more cavalier viewpoint with no church affiliation whatsoever.

That lack of moral compass might have been leading Tom down a path of betrayal, James thought. Miriam seemed very concerned about Elise, and James had seen firsthand Tom and Elise interacting in meetings. It was the kind of thing where Elise finished Tom's sentences for him, and they acted in unison. If the sin hadn't happened yet, the temptation was certainly there. And James would not want the stain of sin on his family name.

Then there were differing political views. James believed fervently that Donald J. Trump was the best president the United States had ever seen. Tom could barely hold his tongue about Trump having damaged democracies worldwide, with a negative impact that would take generations to repair. The two men had to avoid discussing everything from Black Lives Matter and white supremacy to mail-in voting and gun control.

As a committed, ultra-right-wing Republican with aspirations of running for office one day soon, James was keen to maintain his image as a conservative champion within the local party organization. He had always managed to avoid letting anyone in his circle know about his son-in-law's lack of character, and concealing Tom's liberal leanings was of paramount importance to him.

Miriam seemed taken with Patrick McGowan, and if Patrick could get the demons in check that got him fired from

Pellucid, he might be a better overall fit for the family. James thought Patrick losing his job might have served as a wake-up call, and perhaps he could be redeemed since Miriam would be sure to rein him in.

Patrick is a Catholic, but at least he has a church, James thought. Based on prior discussions, it seemed James and Patrick's world views and politics were better aligned.

Yes, things were coming together even if at times it had seemed like everything was disjointed.

Trust in the Lord, James thought, remembering a verse from the Bible's Isaiah 41 that he found inspiring:

> "... *those who oppose you*
> *will be as nothing and perish.*
> *Though you search for your enemies,*
> *you will not find them.*
> *Those who wage war against you*
> *will be as nothing at all."*

The upcoming board meeting will be the battlefield, James mused.

He was looking forward to the opportunity to put some order into the current chaos at Pellucid. His pick for CEO would be an asset and someone James could influence going forward to keep things sweet between Pellucid and his company—and hence the Republican Party.

It's wonderful when the path of righteousness coalesces with personal triumph, James thought, as he started his day by reviewing some of his company's beta trial data derived using Pellucid's software.

 *Chapter 45:*

WINSTON—*DAY 24*—SEPTEMBER 6

Winston was in his office with his door closed and his head in his hands. The guilt and anxiety came in waves, and this was the worst day so far.

A guilty conscience is a strange thing, because just when you're convinced the baggage is shoved down far enough, it pops up again when you least expect it, Winston thought.

No one would believe that "conservative Winston" could have done this, right? Maybe that's what will save me. I can't even believe it, so why would anyone else? But how could I have done this to a friend? I'm not that person! This was so wrong!

Winston's thoughts were swirling because, on top of everything, he had to make this acquisition go through—he had to make this fly.

There was so much to do. Winston realized he'd better snap out of it and get to work.

Chapter 46:

TOM, ELISE, AND LIU—*DAY 25*—SEPTEMBER 7

With Tom getting anxious to leave the safe house, and the impending board meeting three days away, Detective Liu brought Elise back to see Tom and confer on the investigation. When Tom, Elise, and the detective were seated around the small table in the safe house's outdated kitchen, Liu asked Elise to update him on anything she had been able to uncover at Pellucid.

"Something that has changed is Winston," Elise said. "We're used to Winston keeping himself to himself, so to speak. But since Tom supposedly died, I can tell that he is extremely on edge," Elise said. "I've noticed him sitting at his desk looking depressed, which is not surprising since he believes we've lost Tom. But I've also seen him with his head in his hands as if he's in complete despair," Elise continued. "And I heard him talking to someone on his phone in the stairwell when he thought no one was around. He sounded angry and he said if he could, he would turn the clock back."

Liu frowned and made notes in the logbook that seemed to be his trademark.

"Anything else?" Liu asked Elise.

"I've talked to several board members, and we still have two camps on the acquisition. Lawrence and Winston are totally in favor, and I agree it would be a smart move," said Elise.

"On the other side, there is an alliance between Miriam, James, Patrick, and perhaps others who oppose the acquisition. James has been reaching out to the board members, and Patrick has been trying to ingratiate himself with those he got along well with when he was at Pellucid," Elise said.

"Patrick? But he has no vote because he isn't on the board, correct?" Liu asked.

"That's right," Tom responded. "But he may be trying to work his way back into the company now that I'm supposedly out of the picture."

"Is any one of the directors especially adamant about shutting the deal down?" Liu asked.

Tom and Elise looked at each other and said almost simultaneously, "James."

"Why would he be against the acquisition?" Liu asked.

"I'm not a hundred percent sure why he is so opposed, other than he is very controlling and may not want to see Pellucid managed from California. I'm always having to listen to his ideas on running the company as he tries to steer me on things," Tom said, rolling his eyes. "It's awkward, of course, given that he's my father-in-law. He probably assumes correctly that if the company sells, he will have less influence."

"I can imagine that's been a difficult tightrope for you to walk," Liu said, and Tom agreed.

"I should also mention that Miriam has come into the office a couple of times," Elise said.

"What was she doing there?" Liu asked, intrigued.

"Winston said she wanted to run through the current valuation of the company and review the cap table that defines share allocation, and she asked Winston how he would feel about Patrick returning to Pellucid," Elise said quietly, not looking at Tom. "She also said she'll be attending the board meeting this Friday—and something tells me she'll be paying more attention to the proceedings than usual."

"Did she speak with you when she was in?" Liu asked.

"No, Miriam passed by my office but didn't stop in. She's never been friendly with me, and it's been even chillier since Tom has been gone."

Tom got up to make coffee while Liu appeared to be contemplating the latest information. When they all had mugs of coffee in front of them, Liu shared what would happen next.

"Well, good work, Elise, your insights are appreciated. But cards on the table, we're still at a point in the investigation where there's nothing really concrete to act on," said Liu.

"Your supposed death is impeding things, Tom, because we can't interview people freely and tip our hand that you're still alive," Liu explained. "So we're going to have to take a different approach."

"And what does that mean?" Tom asked.

"I'd like you to resurface at the board meeting," Liu concluded.

Chapter 47:

TOM, ELISE, AND LIU MAKE PLANS—*DAY 25*— SEPTEMBER 7

om was excited at the prospect of resuming his life, and he and Elise listened intently as Liu explained how Tom's reappearance would unfold.

"The board meeting will be the perfect opportunity to give us a controlled setting for you to resurface, Tom," Liu said. "I'm hoping that we can leverage the element of surprise to get a read on everyone's reaction, maybe get someone to reveal something when they aren't expecting to see you."

"Well, they'll be surprised, that's for sure! Shocked is probably a better word—especially Miriam," Tom said with some anxiety about the stress this would cause.

"Yes, but unfortunately, we have to pull the Band-Aid off decisively. We need every advantage possible to get closer to finding out the truth about the attacks on you," Liu said, and Tom nodded his agreement.

"So as a starting point, where do you hold your board meetings, and is there a video setup in the room you use?" Liu asked. "I'll need a recording of the meeting and especially the moments after you reappear, Tom."

Tom said Pellucid's board meetings were held at a private members' club, Soho House, on Adelaide Street West, but he wasn't sure about video equipment in the club's library room where they typically met. Liu said he would check and make arrangements if necessary.

Elise suggested that Liu also confirm if Soho House had installed HEPA air purifiers which are specifically designed for indoor venues as a pandemic health precaution. That way, board members could spread out around the table to be socially distanced and feel confident participating in the meeting without wearing masks.

"That's a great point, Elise, as we'll want to be able to clearly see and record everyone's expressions," Liu said. "I'll check into that, and if not, I'll rent some purifier units."

"Aside from the logistics, what's the play-by-play?" Tom asked.

"With Elise being interim co-CEO, she'll be in the room and can give us a heads-up when the time is right for you to show up, Tom," Liu said.

Liu added that he and Tom would wait outside in Liu's car, and Tom would need to wear a baseball cap and sunglasses when going into the building and walking up to the third floor to avoid being recognized by other Soho House patrons. The vintage building had never been equipped with elevators.

"What about Tom's security after the board meeting? Will he still be staying at the safe house until an arrest is made?" Elise asked.

"No, given the pace of the investigation, that's no longer realistic," Liu said, and Tom looked relieved. "I have a meeting with the chief this afternoon to discuss putting a round-the-clock security detail in place, and I have a plan to keep Tom relatively isolated after the safe house."

"I don't expect the city to foot the entire bill for my

protection," Tom interjected. "I can hire a personal security officer through Pellucid. That's no problem."

Liu said he was grateful for the offer and that he could provide Elise with the names of reputable security services that employ former police officers.

"For your safety, it's important for you to stay somewhere that's away from the city and not part of your predictable routine, Tom," Liu said. "I've spoken with Lawrence Cameron, and he's willing to host you at his island cottage near Honey Harbour, which, as you know, is a good two-hour car and boat trip from Toronto.

"It's ideal with the cottage only being accessible by boat, making it challenging for someone to try another attack," Liu continued. "Plus, Lawrence says the cottage has a state-of-the-art security system. And he wanted me to tell you that he's trialing Elon Musk's Starlink service, so you'll have good connectivity to keep the business running from there."

"That sounds like a great plan, Jason, but when did you tell Lawrence I'm alive? Tom asked, surprised at the news.

"I filled him in this morning, and he knows the importance of keeping that strictly confidential until the board meeting on Friday," Liu said. "And, by the way, he got pretty choked up when I told him."

"Oh no! I really feel bad for everyone having to live through this nightmare," Tom said, with a sympathetic glance at Elise. "At least it goes without saying that Lawrence had nothing to do with the attacks?"

"Yes, I'm satisfied that he has no vested interest or motive to want you dead. Quite the contrary," Liu said.

"Ha, what's Lawrence up to now?" Tom said, smiling.

"Lawrence has a US cable news commentator spot lined up, and the successful acquisition by a California company will amp up his authority on American business," Liu said. "He was up front about that with me and said he hadn't told you because he didn't want to influence your decision about the Pellucid acquisition."

Tom chuckled and said, "I always know there can be more to the story with Lawrence." He continued, "What about Miriam? Are you sure we can't prepare her prior to the board meeting? And is the plan for her to come to the cottage with me?"

Liu hesitated and said, "The fewer people who know you're alive prior to the board meeting the better, so no, I'm not comfortable giving Miriam a heads-up. And until we have all the moving parts nailed down, I think it's best if Miriam doesn't go to the cottage with you, Tom. I'm still investigating, and I'd like to restrict the number of people who have access to you in the meantime."

"I'm good with that. As you can imagine, given the Patrick situation, things are awkward for me right now," Tom said. "So we should probably arrange for a hotel room for Miriam to avoid her being hounded by the press after my reappearance," he added, thinking the Four Seasons in Yorkville near Miriam's art gallery would be a good choice. Tom knew from business associates who had stayed there that elevators to guest floors won't operate unless a room key is inserted, making it more secure than the average hotel.

"Elise, can you please book Miriam into the Four Seasons, checking in Friday? Better reserve a two-week stay just in case things don't settle down right away. I'd do it myself, but I'm still dead," Tom quipped, and Elise chuckled as she made a note on her iPhone.

"To your point about news coverage, Tom, Toronto Police will be compelled to be transparent about you being alive. Then it's probably going to be a media feeding frenzy. What are your thoughts on that, Elise?" Liu asked.

"Totally agree," Elise said. "There's no way Tom or Miriam can go home after the news gets out. Reporters would definitely tail them. It's smart for Tom to head out of the city immediately following the board meeting, and Miriam to go straight to the hotel."

Tom said, knowing Miriam, she would insist on getting her things from the house. Elise suggested telling Tom's admin just prior to the meeting that Miriam would be going on a surprise trip with James, and she would need a bag packed and brought to Soho House by the end of the meeting.

"Great idea to solve that problem. And I'll likely need some more things for the cottage as well," Tom noted.

Elise offered to shop for necessities and some new clothes for Tom before Friday.

"Elise, what else do we need to worry about from a media perspective?" Liu asked.

"Social media is so immediate; I'll have to manage that. We can direct board members not to post anything until Tom is on his way to the cottage," Elise said.

Elise said she would contact the Toronto Police Service's corporate communications unit to collaborate on a possible media advisory that could be timed for the conclusion of the board meeting. Regarding requests for more information or interviews, Elise expected those would be declined in view of the ongoing investigation.

"That sounds good, Elise," Liu said. "Can either of you think of anything else we need to address?"

"Yes, if you wouldn't mind helping with something, Jason," Tom said. "I'll need to contact my law firm and let them know I'm not dead. They won't have done anything regarding my will other than preliminary paperwork because they're still waiting for the nonexistent death certificate. But they'll probably want confirmation that this isn't some sort of prank. Can you contact them and confirm officially that I'm still alive? And now that I think of it, could you do the same for our insurance company?"

"Sure, I can do that," Liu said, making note of the law firm and insurance company contact information.

"And Elise, can you call Nate and let him know what's going on after I'm on the road to the cottage? I don't want to freak him out by calling him until he knows I'm alive," Tom said. "I'll call him from the car after you've reached out to him."

"Yes, no problem," Elise said. "Oh, and just one more task for you, Detective: catch Tom's attacker!" Elise added, teasing Liu.

"Ha, that's at the top of my list, Elise," Liu said. "We'll probably be in touch before, but otherwise I'll pick you up at one forty-five on Friday, Tom."

Chapter 48:

TOM, LIU, AND DEREK—*DAY 28*— SEPTEMBER 10

Tom had always been comfortable being a member at Soho House because of the fun, collegial atmosphere of the mostly young entrepreneurs who made up the membership. Some of his colleagues had moved on to other, perhaps more exclusive private member clubs for the sake of networking and business advancement. But Tom came here primarily to unwind and enjoy the company of friends.

As Liu pulled the car over near the Bishop's Building that houses Soho House, Tom was thinking that the third-floor library space was perfect for Pellucid board meetings, with a long, narrow table to accommodate the business portion of the meeting and a beautiful bar for relaxing afterward.

But with this fateful moment drawing nearer, for the first time before a business meeting, Tom felt quite nervous. He was about to shock everyone with his very presence, and that was a big responsibility. And he had no idea what reactions to expect, especially from Miriam and James. His palms were sweaty, and he felt sick at his core for the deception that everyone had suffered since his attack.

Tom's new security officer, Derek, texted that he had just pulled up in an Uber a couple of parking spots behind them. Liu planned to remain downstairs in the lobby of Soho House so he wouldn't distract James and Miriam, who would no doubt recognize him. Derek would accompany Tom upstairs to the meeting, after which Liu would see Tom off to the cottage and then retrieve the video of the proceedings.

Liu gave him a look of encouragement while Tom put on a baseball cap and turned up his collar to avoid recognition and stepped out of the car to join Derek. The moment was at hand.

PART THREE

Chapter 49

TOM AND THE PELLUCID BOARD— SEPTEMBER 10

The board meeting at Soho House got underway as planned on September 10 at two o'clock sharp. As acting chairman and interim co-CEO, Winston was presiding over the meeting.

"Good afternoon, everyone, and thank you for coming today," Winston said, looking out at the board members seated around the expansive table. Winston stood at the front of the room under a digital presentation screen. Elise was seated to his right, also facing the other board members.

Above the digital screen, the video camera had been activated with a clear view of all participants. The entrance to the room was at the back. As planned, the air purifiers were in place, so no one felt compelled to wear a mask.

Winston continued, "This is the most solemn board meeting that we have ever had, given the passing of our CEO and dear friend Tom Oliver. I know it's difficult to conduct 'business as usual,' but Tom of all people would have wanted Pellucid to continue to thrive. And so here we are.

"I would particularly like to welcome Miriam and thank her for attending, given the circumstances," Winston said, and the group applauded.

"I would also like to recognize Elise for her focus and dedication as we've been serving as co-CEOs. I couldn't have made it through without her collaboration," Winston said, smiling at Elise, which elicited more applause.

Elise acknowledged the recognition and then discreetly sent a text message from her phone saying, *It's time.*

"Now, if you could turn your attention to the screen, here is today's agenda. As a level set, I'd like us to take a quick look back at a media interview Tom did in July. Then we'll review the cap table and have discussion on that, followed by consideration of candidates for the CEO role," Winston said.

At that moment, Tom entered the room. The board members didn't see him coming in from the back of the room but Winston, who was facing Tom, looked as if he might fall over.

"Tom!" Winston exclaimed.

Tom was behind Miriam so she couldn't see him, but Miriam could see Elise, and Elise's face registered not surprise, but delight. When Miriam turned and saw Tom, she paled but quickly regained her composure, leaping from her seat to throw her arms around her husband in a show of loyalty.

Tom kissed Miriam on the top of her head and then removed her arms gently, sat her back down, mouthing, "I can explain," as he walked to the front of the room.

There was stunned silence until he said, "Hi, everyone. You can believe your eyes. It's really me."

Winston stared at Tom in amazement and said, "Holy shit, Tom, welcome back," and everyone laughed and jumped up to clap and cheer.

In a few minutes, Winston tapped his coffee mug like a gavel.

"Everyone, let's give Tom some breathing room here and

let him tell us how this is even possible," Winston said. "Tom, you have the floor."

Tom acknowledged Elise with a smile as he moved to the center of the boardroom table, underneath the video camera.

"Thank you all for welcoming me back to life so enthusiastically," Tom said, making eye contact with each person seated around the table, especially Miriam and James. "You can't imagine how wonderful it is to see all of you. I apologize that you have been through an extremely difficult time. And I'm sincerely sorry to just show up like this and surprise everyone—most of all you, Miriam.

"But the deception was for a good reason. I need to share with you that there have been a couple of attempts on my life, and the Toronto Police Service took extraordinary steps to ensure my safety.

"The 'accident' in Caledon was not a riding incident but rather a planned attack. Someone struck me viciously when I stopped to check a boobytrap. I sustained lacerations to my neck and I'm told that I'm lucky the murder attempt wasn't successful."

Tom waited a moment for the group to absorb what he had just said.

"The police thought it best for me to be declared dead and protected in a safe house while they got to the bottom of things. Unfortunately, that meant absolutely no one could know that I'm alive. And we still don't know who did this or, perhaps more importantly, why. At this point in the investigation, they felt it was time for me to reemerge.

"I'm truly sorry for the pain and anxiety this has caused everyone," Tom said, looking at Miriam in particular. "And hopefully the police will have the mystery solved soon so we can put this chapter behind us.

"In the meantime, I'll introduce my security officer, Derek Jones. He is the fellow who just joined us, standing at the back of the room insistent on wearing a suit—so I feel like I've got a personal bouncer," Tom quipped.

When heads turned in his direction, Derek nodded to the group.

"Derek is going to ensure my ongoing security now that I'm out of the safe house. The city has done more than its part to protect and defend, so Pellucid's operational budget is covering Derek's services.

"Well, enough about me! I'd like to thank Winston and Elise for their hard work as acting co-CEOs in my absence. Elise, I'm sure my reappearance is going to cause you a media relations nightmare to manage, but as usual, I know we can rely on you to handle it well," Tom said.

"I do need to caution everyone not to share my return with anyone outside this room," he continued. "No social posts please until Miriam and I have relocated to undisclosed locations for privacy and safety's sake later today."

At that, Miriam looked shocked—and annoyed.

"Winston, I'm sorry to disrupt your agenda for the day, but here's what I'm thinking," Tom said. "The agenda items related to allocation of shares and selection of a new CEO can be taken off the table since I'm still here.

"As to the rest of the agenda, I move that we set aside the discussion on the acquisition until a later date. Crystal Clere's original date for our decision on the acquisition was September 15. But if I'm correct, the agenda states that they have extended the deadline to the thirtieth given our situation, is that right, Winston?"

Winston nodded and said, "Yes, correct."

Tom continued, "So let's schedule our next meeting for September 27, which gives us time to complete all due diligence work and determine our final response before the deadline."

"That also gives me time to get fully back into the saddle so to speak and to reconnect with all of you. I move that we deal with immediate business, table the acquisition review, and open the bar."

"I'll second that!" Winston said with gusto.

When a few routine orders of business had been dealt with, the board meeting was adjourned and everyone moved from the table to the bar area, with lots of laughter and chatter releasing the tension of the last month. Meanwhile, Tom took Miriam to a private office on the next floor down so they could catch up properly.

 *Chapter 50:*

TOM AND MIRIAM—SEPTEMBER 10

"**I**'m so mad at you! You've been alive all this time, and I've gone through hell and beyond in the meantime, and you're just fine?" Miriam exclaimed when the door shut behind them.

"Well, if you call almost being killed twice 'just fine,' then I suppose you have a point," Tom responded.

"And you couldn't have let me know you are still alive before this circus in front of the whole board?" Miriam said angrily. "I'm surprised I didn't faint and make a fool of myself."

"No, the police had their reasons for doing things this way," said Tom.

"We had a memorial service, Tom. And a reading of the will, of all things! This is so embarrassing. What am I supposed to tell people?" Miriam fussed, starting to pace the floor.

"Embarrassing?" Tom said incredulously. "Seriously, that's what you're thinking about right now?" Tom shook his head in disbelief. "Look, I'm truly sorry for everything you've been through, Miriam, but as I explained, I was following police direction. And this was the second attempt on my life in a couple of weeks, one of which put me in hospital."

Miriam's eyes widened. "Am I in any danger?"

"No. I have absolutely no idea who did this or why—but I seem to have been the only target," Tom said, marveling at Miriam's predictable instinct for self-preservation.

When her temper subsided and she'd absorbed the situation, Miriam gathered herself and asked, "So were your injuries really bad?"

"Well, it wasn't the best time I've ever had," Tom said. He leaned forward and showed her the lacerations on his neck, and Miriam gasped. "I was lucky though, as it could have been much worse."

"Oh, Tom, I'm so sorry." And Miriam gave him a sincere hug.

"Miriam, I appreciate that, but I'm also aware of everything that's happened in the last few weeks."

Miriam's spine stiffened and she looked at him defiantly, stepping back. "What does that mean?"

"I mean Patrick," Tom said. "I'm aware that you've moved on. And I'm not blaming you. I know you thought I was dead."

"I saw you on screen with my own eyes, Tom. Yes, I believed you were dead," Miriam said defensively.

"Well, to be honest, Miriam," Tom said gently, "I think you and I both know that things were coming apart for us, even before all this happened. Maybe this was the catalyst we needed to make a change."

"Oh, how convenient," Miriam said sarcastically. "So you and Elise can get on with things."

"What?" Tom said. "Miriam, there has never been anything inappropriate between Elise and me. Unlike you and Patrick—going back as far as the party at Lawrence's cottage, I believe. Maybe earlier?"

"You can't tell me that Elise didn't know you were alive before this meeting. I saw her face today, and she wasn't shocked," Miriam said bitterly.

"Look, I don't think we're going to solve anything by trading accusations, and we need to talk more another time," Tom said. "I've had lots of time to think, while you've just been hit with this crazy turn of events. So this isn't fair to you."

Miriam was quiet and looked away.

"I'm honestly happy to see you again, Miriam, and I have nothing but good thoughts about our life together. I hope you'll be able to forgive me for what you've been through," Tom said, reaching out unsuccessfully to take her hand.

At that point, there was a knock at the door. Predictably, it was James.

James looked as angry as Miriam, but he maintained his decorum when he challenged Tom.

"I have zero respect for how this has been handled, Tom. Zero respect. I'm disappointed in what Toronto calls a police department, I'm disappointed in you for going along with this charade, and I'm very, very angry that you treated my daughter so shamefully," James said. "I'm glad you have your health back, but this is just unforgivable."

James stood beside Miriam with his right arm sheltering her as if she needed protection from Tom, and Tom could only offer the same explanation and apology that he had given to Miriam.

Tom moved things along and shared the arrangements that had been made for Miriam to avoid publicity. He also assured James that hotel security had been apprised of the need for Miriam's privacy because of the expected media interest, and he advised her to maintain a low profile for at least the next few days.

"Where are you going to be, back at the safe house?" Miriam asked.

"No, the police have arranged a different place for me to stay for a while, just until this all blows over," Tom said.

"More secrecy, I suppose," said Miriam in a huff.

"You can always reach me, Miriam. I'll have my phone with me," Tom said.

As Miriam turned to leave the room with her father, Tom knew it would be some time before she would be able to process everything. And sadly, neither Miriam nor James was likely to ever forgive him for keeping them in the dark.

When Miriam and James had left, Tom joined the other directors upstairs to catch up and answer questions about the attempted murder investigation. Then Tom, Lawrence, and Derek headed outside to a waiting limo and headed north to the cottage, while Liu went to his office with the video footage in hand.

 *Chapter 51:*

ELISE—SEPTEMBER 10

Pellucid board members were thrilled to have Tom back and buoyantly celebrated his reappearance. Before Tom left, the group had peppered him with questions about his injuries, what being at the safe house had been like, whether he thought the acquisition was still viable, and more—until Elise had cautioned that Tom still needed to take care and that was probably enough for one day.

As the gathering dispersed, Elise wished everyone a great weekend but reminded the team not to comment on social media nor respond to media queries.

Winston went to the Pellucid office to share the good news with staff and to close early so employees would not be approached by reporters when the news broke.

The Toronto Police Service corporate communications unit had collaborated with Elise as planned to prepare the advisory that would be distributed on the Greater Toronto Area PR news-wire at three thirty. They had agreed that only the basic facts would be provided, and neither the police nor Pellucid would comment. Journalists would be directed to the advisory posted on both the police and Pellucid websites, and interviews would be declined on the basis that "this is still an active investigation."

With the meeting over, the office closed and locked securely by Winston, and Tom on the way to the cottage, Elise went to her condo—with no plans to venture out for the entire weekend. Elise updated her voicemail to refer reporters to the Pellucid website and prepared to monitor social media.

The advisory crossed the wire right on time:

Media Advisory—for Immediate Distribution
3:30 p.m. ET

TORONTO—September 10, 2021—The Toronto Police Service today announced that 38-year-old Tom Oliver, CEO of Toronto-based software company Pellucid, is alive and well, having recovered from serious injuries sustained in an attack that occurred August 14, 2021, in Caledon, Ontario.

It was reported at the time that Oliver had died as the result of an equestrian accident. Oliver was, in fact, the victim of attempted murder. Taking into consideration all aspects of the case, the Toronto Police Service placed Oliver, with his consent, in a safe house where he has remained until today.

There have been no arrests to date in this case. Due to the ongoing investigation, the Toronto Police Service is unable to provide any further information on the incident. Oliver and family are at an undisclosed location and are unavailable for comment.

It took no time at all before Tom Oliver and Pellucid were trending on Twitter, and the fallout wasn't good:

"Pellucid's CEO rises from the dead—what the hell?"

"Toronto Police spend taxpayer money protecting CEO and still don't know whodunit!"

"Guess you get preferential protection when you're the son of a former top cop!"

"Wait—did the horse try to kill the guy? Black Beauty is now Cujo?"

CP24 ran the story on their continuous TV news broadcast, which would catch the attention of commuters waiting for their trains at Union Station. Elise was grateful that Lawrence could provide a safe haven for Tom while the media storm blew up across the city.

Thank goodness it's Friday! Maybe by Monday there will be other breaking news to deflect attention away from Pellucid, Elise thought hopefully.

 *Chapter 52:*

TOM AND LAWRENCE—SEPTEMBER 10

om was exhilarated but emotionally drained after the events of the afternoon. He was glad to have a comfortable limo ride out of Toronto, away from the safe house and all the controversy, and grateful to have Lawrence's companionship after such a long time on his own. Derek was sitting up front with the driver, giving Tom and Lawrence some needed privacy.

There was one more piece of important business that needed to be handled immediately before the news reached Silicon Valley: advising Crystal Clere's CEO that Tom was still alive. It was early afternoon in California, so they were able to catch the CEO just as he returned from lunch. Lawrence spoke to him first and explained what had just transpired, and then Tom advised that he was doing well and would be back at the helm of Pellucid. Expressing relief and feeling reassured, the CEO committed to sending the letter of intent that afternoon, which was the best news Tom had received in a long time.

As Tom and Lawrence were catching up on things in the limo, Elise texted that she had called Nate, who was surprised— but not effusive—about Tom still being alive.

Tom then called Nate, and they had their usual strained interaction, despite what should have been happy news. Nate asked for the details of what had happened, and Tom told him about the boobytrap placed across his path and being attacked.

Following Tom's call with Nate, Lawrence recommended that Tom stay off social media and ignore any commentary swirling after the media advisory being issued.

"Elise will keep us updated on anything we need to know, and why cause yourself more stress over something you can't control?" Lawrence said. He had noticed Tom was tiring after dealing with Miriam and James. And after all, it hadn't been that long since his injuries had healed.

Tom was grateful for Lawrence's counsel and closed his eyes for a nap on the way to the cottage, where a meal prepared by Lawrence's personal chef would be waiting. Tom was looking forward to sleeping in a comfortable bed and waking up to the stunning view of the granite cliffs across the channel.

Chapter 53:

ELISE—SEPTEMBER 11

Elise woke up early on Saturday, anxious to search for news coverage or social media commentary that might have appeared after she had finally disengaged at midnight. Her heart jumped when the *Toronto Star* headline popped up on her laptop:

> *"Attacker rigged trap for Pellucid CEO Tom Oliver, brother reports."*

And a subhead:

> *"Police searching for GoPro with video of the attacker."*

"His stupid, useless brother!" Elise exclaimed out loud.

Tom had told Elise he'd talked to Nate, but she wasn't aware that he had shared any details of the case. Nate must have wasted no time contacting the *Star* and spilling everything he knew—which wasn't much.

Just enough to make it sound exclusive, Elise fumed.

The article quoted Nate who said, "The police may have a video of the person who attacked my brother. Tom attaches a GoPro to his riding helmet, and if he was wearing it that day, they'll have footage."

So Tom hadn't told him anything about the video. Nate was just laying it on thick with anything he could to embellish the story, Elise realized.

Oh, this is really something! she thought as she read more of the story.

Nate had elaborated, saying, "My brother could do no wrong, and I was the one who took all the abuse in the family. I don't mean physical abuse, just the brunt of any criticism. Tom and I had totally different experiences growing up, and no one knows that side of things. They just know me as the black sheep because that's what they've been told."

What a nightmare! It's not bad enough that Tom's fake death hit the news, but now this! Elise thought. *And there's no point telling Nate to stop giving interviews. No doubt he loves being center stage while his brother can't comment. He's having a terrific time at Tom and Pellucid's expense!*

It reminded Elise of Meghan Markle's opportunistic father talking to the media any chance he got. *So petty when relatives do this.*

As she was contemplating letting Tom know the latest, the phone rang.

"Detective Liu, how are you? Yes, I've seen the story.

"Yes, Nate is a huge liability.

"No, I have no concerns about anyone else on the board or Pellucid staff saying anything. I've advised everyone not to give interviews, and they will put Tom first. I think Nate— and possibly Patrick—are the only ones motivated to speak to the media.

"I'm sorry this happened, and Tom is going to be furious with Nate, that's for sure.

"Okay. Thanks for calling."

Elise would wait a little longer before calling Tom to update him. It was only 7:30 a.m., and she hoped he would have a chance to sleep in at the cottage.

Chapter 54:

LIU AND THE CRIMINAL PSYCHOLOGIST—
SEPTEMBER 11

Detective Liu was not in a good mood this Saturday morning. He had been made aware from the top of the police service that the case needed solving pronto in view of all the media attention stirred up by Tom's reappearance. Toronto Police were coming under considerable criticism for providing such extensive protection for a private citizen—regardless of family connections—with no tangible results.

And that self-serving ass Nate talking to the media when he knew nothing—plus managing to drop disparaging comments about Tom into interviews—was beyond annoying. Nate had referenced being abandoned by his brother after his parents died and portrayed himself as the much-maligned younger child in an ambitious family.

It was all about Nate, not his brother who was attacked, Liu thought, disgusted with Nate's callous attitude.

Liu was also disgruntled because working Saturdays had become the norm instead of an exception.

"Not that anyone would appreciate it." Liu grumbled to himself as he grabbed an espresso to jump-start his day.

Today he was meeting with an expert on criminal behavior, a psychologist on call for police work, and they would be reviewing the case and in particular the boardroom video. Maybe she would have some insight with fresh eyes on the case.

Liu stood up from his desk to greet Dr. Nancy Carruthers. They hadn't met before, but he had heard good things about her expertise, and she had helped crack a complex homicide case the previous year. With long gray hair swept up into a bun, wire-rimmed glasses, and a paisley-patterned scarf wrapped around her shoulders, she matched Liu's stereotypical picture of a psych expert.

After making their introductions and running through the facts of the investigation, which took little time because Dr. Carruthers had done her homework reviewing the file, Liu noted, they were ready to watch the boardroom video.

"What I would suggest, Detective, is watching the meeting in its entirety and then more closely examining each person's reaction to Tom's reappearance," said Dr. Carruthers.

Liu agreed, and while they viewed the video, Dr. Carruthers took copious notes—*a woman after my own heart*, Liu thought, given his propensity for note-taking. Then it was time to discuss her impressions.

The analysis started with Winston, who chaired the meeting and was the first to see Tom enter the room. The video didn't capture Winston's facial expression, as his back was to the camera, but Dr. Carruthers noted the genuine surprise in his voice and the fact that he had to steady himself with a hand on the table. He had certainly been shocked at Tom's return.

"That doesn't mean anything in terms of motivation or involvement, however, since even the attacker would have thought Tom was dead," Dr. Carruthers noted.

They skipped over Elise as a suspect since Liu had ruled her out, but Dr. Carruthers did remark that Elise's body language—leaning forward eagerly as Tom arrived—spoke volumes about how she felt about him.

The next person of interest was Miriam's father, James Robinson. Dr. Carruthers spent considerable time reviewing his reaction to Tom's arrival and his body language and behavior throughout the board meeting.

"This man does not look happy to see Tom. He looks angry, even frustrated, not the reaction that one would expect from a fellow board member and especially a father-in-law. James rose from his chair more slowly than others when everyone stood to cheer for Tom, and he frequently looked at his daughter as if he were checking in on her. I want to come back to him again when we've finished running through the main players."

Liu nodded and brought up the footage of Miriam when Tom showed up.

"Miriam is an interesting one," Dr. Carruthers continued. "Winston yelled, 'Tom!' but Miriam didn't immediately turn around. Instead, she froze for a moment, and she was looking right at Elise at the front of the room. That hesitation tells me that she was more interested in how another woman responded to seeing Tom than his actual reappearance.

"I would have to conclude there is some history there, some resentment, perhaps a rift in Miriam and Tom's marriage. Miriam's reaction to her husband returning from the dead was not what one might expect. She is very reserved, with no tears, no 'I love you.' And like her father, she was slow to join the ovation for Tom. But to be fair, she is clearly in shock, and if she's an introverted person, this may be as demonstrative as she gets.

"Lawrence, of course, doesn't look surprised at all, because you had filled him in before the meeting. The whole time he watches Tom speak to the board, he looks like a proud father whose child just made the honor roll. I think your judgment that Lawrence is a Tom supporter and an unlikely suspect is astute, Detective."

Dr. Carruthers replayed the video of James reacting to Tom's entrance multiple times. "I do find James Robinson especially interesting," she said. "There is something there, a reason he doesn't want Tom back in the picture, perhaps. I would recommend looking into that further, Detective."

"Tom has shared with me that his father-in-law does his best to pull all the strings at Pellucid, so he might have felt more empowered with Tom gone," Liu said. "He and Tom don't have much in common, so there's a strained family dynamic as well."

Dr. Carruthers nodded understanding and said, "That could explain what I'm seeing. From the case notes, I gather James enjoys a fair bit of influence over Miriam, and it probably annoyed him that he didn't have as much success trying to steer Tom."

"Yes, I think that's a big part of the issue," Liu agreed.

Dr. Carruthers ran through all the board members in attendance, and there were no anomalies to report in anyone else's reaction. She did have an interesting observation to make about the group, however.

"It strikes me what an impressive group of people this is," she said. "They are power people, intelligent, well-educated, well-dressed, affluent, successful, in their prime. These are people accustomed to working hard, perhaps, but not in the traditional get-your-hands-dirty sense.

"These are the type of people who might not be capable of committing a crime themselves, but they would have the means, if they were so inclined, to hire someone to do the dirty work."

Her words resonated with Liu, who was having a difficult time ascribing the crime to any of them.

"If it's not presumptuous on my part, Detective, I would say the killer-for-hire theory might be worth checking out," Dr. Carruthers noted. Maybe it's time to draft warrants to obtain documents and information on the finances of anyone sufficiently suspect. It could be interesting to find out if any big payouts have been made in the right timeframe.

"What's the going rate for a hired killer these days?" Dr. Carruthers asked, only half joking, as she put away her notebook.

Liu felt a chill, something that tended to happen when a case was moving forward.

"Before you go, Dr. Carruthers, can I ask you about a couple of people who weren't in attendance at the board meeting?" Liu asked.

"Of course," Dr. Carruthers said, looking intrigued.

"Tom Oliver has a brother, Nate, who is four years younger and much less successful. His path has included substance abuse, not-great jobs, and a trail of broken relationships. After Tom shared that he was still alive, Nate immediately did a media interview that resulted in a tell-all front-page story in the *Star*. My question for you is why would this guy do that, knowing his brother may still be at risk?"

"My first inclination would be that Nate is a classic narcissist, looking for attention at any cost. At the extreme end of the scale, self-centeredness can mean an inability to empathize with or even love others. He may have no feelings other than resentment for his brother.

"If he is both a narcissist and a sociopath, he may not just be a harmless, foolish fellow wanting to see himself in the media. I would say he is definitely worth further investigation, Detective."

Liu made some notes on that point and then said, "The other person of concern is Patrick McGowan. He's a former friend of Tom's, recently fired from a lucrative post at Tom's company, Pellucid. McGowan is a bit of an athlete, certainly strong enough to attack someone physically, reputed to have a hot temper at times. From all accounts, he is furious with Tom for being let go from Pellucid, made worse by the fact the company has amazing opportunities coming up."

Dr. Carruthers was thoughtful for a moment.

"I can see why he could be top of mind when you're looking at suspects, Detective, and sometimes the obvious is the right answer. But if he did come after Tom, it seems to me he would have tried to hide his resentment and act publicly as if it were no big deal to be fired. He sounds like an emotionally-driven man, and that makes me think he would be more likely to commit a crime of passion in the moment than a planned attack," said Dr. Carruthers. "But that's not to say he doesn't warrant further investigation if you have any concerns."

"This has all been very helpful, Doctor," Liu said. "Can I call on you again if need be?"

"Of course, it would be my pleasure," Dr. Carruthers said.

When she had left, Liu sat back and reviewed his suspect board again. Perhaps these interconnected people were finally coming into some sort of focus. Liu had a lot of work to do, including getting a couple of warrants moving.

 *Chapter 55:*

LIU AND PATRICK—SEPTEMBER 13

A forensics report had landed on Liu's desk confirming that bits of plastic found at the Caledon attack scene matched the model of Tom's GoPro. That was useful to corroborate Tom's statement, which at least provided something concrete.

And investigating officers reported to Liu that Patrick McGowan had purchased wire at a farm supply store in Caledon the week before the attack on Tom.

That was the clincher for Liu, who decided to start his week by bringing McGowan in for questioning. He was already suspicious because McGowan drove a black BMW like the one in the Yorkville incident, and he had cause to want Tom dead given his interest in both Miriam and no doubt her money as well. Liu planned to find out where McGowan was at the time of the two murder attempts and how he would explain buying wire.

An officer had picked up McGowan, and he was now seated in an interview room, clearly annoyed at being brought into the station. Looking into the interview room through one-way glass, Liu could see McGowan's increasing agitation.

"Mr. McGowan, thanks for coming in," Liu said when he entered the small room.

"Did I have a choice?" Patrick retorted.

"Not really," Liu said, trying to put him at ease with a smile. "Did anyone offer you coffee?"

"No, but thanks, I'm good. Can we just get on with this?" he said.

"Sure. You probably realize this is related to the recent attack on your former employer, Tom Oliver," Liu stated.

"I assumed so," Patrick said.

"I need to ask, where were you the night of July 29?" Liu queried.

"I have no idea. Can I look at my phone a minute to refresh my memory?" Patrick asked.

"Sure," Liu said.

Patrick looked at his calendar and said, "Oh yes, I often connect with some mates on Zoom to watch rugby and chat during the game, and we were watching our favorite team play against Brazil that night."

"What time would that have been?" Liu said.

McGowan's response gave him a solid alibi for the time of the Yorkville attempt on Tom, Liu thought. That is, if it checked out. He asked McGowan for the names of a couple of his friends who could corroborate his statement.

"And on the day of the Caledon attack on Tom, August 14, where were you then?" Liu asked.

"You can't seriously think I had anything to do with this!" Patrick said angrily, his face turning slightly red.

"We have to investigate all avenues," Liu said calmly. "Can you tell me where you were that Saturday morning?"

"If you must know, I had a date the night before with a very lovely woman, and I stayed over. So that morning I was still at her place," Patrick said.

Liu could see that McGowan was incensed. No doubt he realized that a police officer would need to verify his alibi with this woman whom he was probably only casually dating.

"What else do you have for me, Detective?" Patrick asked, his impatience now on full display.

Liu then broached the question of McGowan having bought wire prior to the attack on Tom.

"Oh, bloody hell, that was wire to attach corner posts for a pigpen I was building at the stable where Tom, Elise, and I keep our horses," Patrick said.

"A pigpen?" Liu raised his eyebrows.

"Yes, damned potbellied pig, if you must know," Patrick said.

Liu made note of the explanation and then asked McGowan a final question.

"Do you know of anyone who would want Tom dead or who could benefit from his death?" Liu asked.

The question seemed to throw McGowan off a bit, Liu thought, since he felt under the gun himself for the crimes.

"The only person I've encountered in the time I've known Tom who would have enough animosity to do something like that would be his brother, Nate," Patrick said. "Nate is an odd guy, keeps to himself, and has always resented Tom, from what I can tell."

"That's all for now. Thank you for your time, Mr. McGowan. If anything else comes up, we'll be in touch," Liu said.

"I'm sure you will," Patrick said sarcastically as he strode out of the room, looking like a man in need of a rugby scrum to take out his frustrations.

Back to the drawing board, Liu thought as he closed the door.

 *Chapter 56:*

TOM—SEPTEMBER 13

Lawrence's cottage seemed a world away from the turmoil Tom had left behind in Toronto following his reappearance at the board meeting. Surrounded by Canadian Shield granite rock outcroppings, dense forest, and deep blue waters, the island enclave offered an idyllic setting. Tom had spent the weekend relaxing with Lawrence and Grace, who were the kindest of hosts. Grace insisted on treating him and Derek like members of the extended family, so they were all enjoying excellent food and drink.

Now, with the start of a new work week, Tom planned to make progress on the acquisition. He needed to review the letter of intent, which he had received as promised from Crystal Clere's CEO, and to discuss the terms of the offer with Winston and their lawyer. Tom would then collaborate with Winston to complete their assessment and prepare for the board's vote.

It would be important at this critical juncture to ensure that Winston was on his game and ready to complete the due diligence. Elise's observation that the inscrutable Winston was preoccupied and stressed concerned Tom, and he had no idea why there had been such a shift in Winston's demeanor.

As Tom was mulling over how to broach an open discussion with Winston, his phone rang. Ironically, it was Winston asking to meet with Tom in person as soon as possible. Tom explained that he was staying at Lawrence's cottage and that Winston needed to keep his location confidential. As Winston was happy to drive up to Honey Harbour the next day, Tom said he would arrange to have a water taxi waiting to bring Winston from the town dock to the cottage.

Tom was cognizant of Liu's input that anyone could be a suspect, so he let Liu know about the meeting and assured him that his security officer would be on duty.

With that key meeting arranged, Tom had just one more pressing issue to address: his brother's betrayal.

 *Chapter 57:*

TOM AND NATE—SEPTEMBER 13

The media hype over Tom's reappearance had continued all weekend, and Tom was well aware that Nate had contributed to that. Tom knew that he needed to broach what his father would have called a come-to-Jesus meeting with his brother to discuss his egregious comments in interviews—and avoid further damaging coverage.

Tom calculated the best time for a call, when Nate would be at home but would have had insufficient opportunity to get drunk. Nate picked up on the fourth ring. "Hey, Nate, it's Tom."

Silence. Long pause.

"What do you want?" Nate said sourly.

"I thought we could talk about a few things," Tom said.

"Like what?" Nate growled.

"Well, for starters, the stuff you told the media about our family wasn't particularly helpful right now. I trust you're aware that although I didn't die, I was severely injured in the attack?"

"As far as I'm concerned, all I did was tell the truth," Nate said defiantly.

Typical. Nate couldn't care less that I was badly injured and might still be in danger, Tom thought.

Nate reiterated his viewpoint that he had been treated like a second-rate citizen by their parents, always paling in comparison to Tom. He also brought up the issue of Tom having left for England after their parents' death for perhaps the thousandth time. Tom's patience was wearing thin with Nate always playing the victim.

"Look, Nate, you know I had already enrolled for my master's before Mom and Dad died. I didn't have a lot of resources back then and I would have lost the tuition money if I canceled at the eleventh hour. And you always pushed me away, anyway, so what was the point of staying in Canada?"

"Ya, sure, it's never your fault, is it?" Nate snapped.

"Oh, for Christ's sake, at this point can we get past whose fault it is and just look at the facts? You're thirty-four years old, you have skills, especially your ability as an artist, and isn't it time you took responsibility for yourself?" Tom snapped back.

"Easy for you to say. Have you heard the expression *starving artist*? Ask your precious wife how much help she's been as a gallery curator," Nate said sarcastically. "That woman is a snob."

"Don't take things out on Miriam!" Tom said, feeling his blood pressure climbing.

The conversation had fallen into the same continuous loop that had linked the two men for much of their lives. Tom tried a different approach.

"Nate, the bottom line for me is that you and I have no living relatives besides each other, except for our distant cousins. I'd like my one immediate family member to be someone I can count on and who can count on me. But it can't be a one-way street where you just come to me when you need money. And you can't expect me to have your back if you don't have mine. That's not a relationship," Tom said.

"I'm not sure where you got the idea I want a relationship with you, Tom. And I think you owe me big time after all the crap I've been through while you've been living in style," Nate said.

Tom sighed, and there was a long silence between them.

"If all you want is money, then I'm prepared to make you a generous offer, Nate. But I need to be clear that I'm done with the guilt trips, the public putdowns, and the harassment for money. If I give you a settlement, that's it. We agree that it's a one-time gift, and you are free to do your own thing without keeping in touch if that's what you want," Tom said. "But in return, you have to agree to stop behaving like a jerk and disparaging our family."

Nate was quiet for a few minutes.

"I can do that," Nate said.

"Fine. I'll have my lawyer put in place the trust fund that would have been bequeathed in my will."

"That's big of you," Nate said, and hung up.

Tom was profoundly sad when the connection dropped, but he realized this was reality. He could almost hear his mother's voice saying, "It is what it is, Tommy. That's Nate. Time to move on."

Chapter 58:

WINSTON—SEPTEMBER 14

I f Winston hadn't been feeling tied up in knots about what he had to do next, he would have been able to fully enjoy the scenery on the boat ride from the Honey Harbour marina to Lawrence's cottage.

Tree-laden cliffs rising from the water's edge framed the incredibly blue waters of Georgian Bay. Some of the trees already had a tinge of fall color, turning shades of yellow and red in a precursor to autumn.

The water taxi pulled into the channel that ran in front of Lawrence's cottage.

One should say "so-called cottage," because this place is more like a mansion on the water, Winston thought.

Tiered decking and patios led upward from the dock, and stone steps ascended to a rambling post-and-beam-style dwelling with multiple balconies. With the exterior of the cottage featuring stone and wood, the structure integrated unobtrusively into the island landscape. Dockage to accommodate deep-water boats jutted out into the water, making the "cottage" look more like a marine resort than a private complex.

Such a beautiful day for such a difficult task, Winston thought, bracing himself for what he had to do as he stepped onto the dock.

There to meet him was security officer Derek, looking intimidating.

Chapter 59:

TOM, WINSTON, AND DEREK—SEPTEMBER 14

om decided to meet with Winston on the lower terrace, one level up from the dock, where Lawrence's housekeeper had set out coffee and pastries on a serving table. It felt a little like they were meeting somewhere on the Mediterranean, with deck chairs on the terrace and a white linen tablecloth billowing in the breeze.

He watched from above as Derek waited at the dock for the water taxi to tie up. When Winston stepped off, Derek asked him to open his jacket and show him what was in his pockets. Winston had a computer bag with him, which Derek inspected. Tom thought how bizarre it was to have to suspect everyone, even his trusted business associates. When Derek gave Winston the all-clear, the two men walked up to the terrace.

"Tom, how are you?" Winston asked, as they greeted each other with a COVID elbow bump.

"I'm good, thanks. I'm definitely enjoying Lawrence's hospitality and especially being out of the safe house," Tom said, smiling. "It's probably still freaking you out that I'm actually here—something like dead man walking, right?"

"Yes, no kidding, it's pretty surreal," Winston said.

After Tom offered him coffee, the two men settled in on large Muskoka chairs facing the water. Derek sat behind them, but close enough to take action if need be.

Winston appeared to be way beyond stressed.

He looks like he's going to have a heart attack or maybe just implode on the spot, Tom thought, puzzled about what could be the issue.

"Tom, I don't know where to begin, but I won't blame you if, at the end of our discussion, you want me to tender my resignation," Winston said quietly, hoping Derek couldn't hear the conversation.

"Wow. Well, let's treat this as a safe space where you can say your piece, Winston, and we'll go from there," Tom said calmly.

Winston nodded, took a deep breath, and began.

"It's going to come to light very soon that there's a hundred thousand dollars unaccounted for in Pellucid's cash flow," Winston said.

"Go on," Tom said.

"To cut to the chase, I've done something incredibly stupid that has an impact on the company," Winston said. "At the beginning of the summer, a friend of mine came to me with what he considered a bulletproof pre-IPO offer for a stock in the health care sector.

"The company was involved in making psychedelic drugs for legitimate treatment purposes and had a division that was on the brink of having an instant test for COVID variants. With two hot sectors covered, my friend felt this would take off, and I bought in.

"I didn't have the cash available in my own account— to be honest, I had just bought the condo on the waterfront and all my money was tied up in that—so I gave myself a temporary loan from Pellucid."

Winston paused, and Tom knew his expression had telegraphed the shock he was feeling.

"I know now that it was foolish—and wrong—but I was convinced it would just be a month or so before I'd double my money and could replace the loan," Winston said. "I should have talked to you about it and gone about this the right way, and for that, I'm very sorry."

"And let me guess. The IPO didn't net what they expected?" Tom said.

"The day after the IPO, the Federal Drug Administration in the US declined use of the instant test because it hit a roadblock in advance trials," Winston said. "The timing couldn't have been worse, and instead of going up from their issue price, the stock has tanked."

"If you sell the shares you bought into now, what would you net?" Tom asked.

"Thirty thousand," Winston said, mortified at the loss. "And I wish I could tell you that I can make good on the seventy thousand, but right now I don't have it."

Tom was aware that Winston had been sending money to his sister for his nieces' education fund, so he probably hadn't been in the best financial position even before his condo purchase.

"I assume that you didn't record the loan in any reporting to shareholders or on the books yet?" Tom said.

"No, but it has to be shown on the upcoming month-end report," Winston said.

"And this was within your signing limit of two-hundred fifty thousand, so it wouldn't look unusual except for the purpose the money was used for?" Tom noted.

"Yes, that's right. No one else had to be involved in signing this off, so I am solely to blame. And I can't tell you how sorry I am for taking a risk with Pellucid funds and having it turn out this way," Winston said.

Tom could barely believe what he was hearing because it was so out of character for Winston. Winston had always been the voice of financial reason and had never steered him wrong on business moves. Tom considered Winston to be a huge asset to the company for the very reason of his conservative financial stewardship. And now this.

No wonder Winston has been in turmoil over how to make things right, Tom thought.

"I'm very grateful to have the opportunity to tell you man-to-man what happened, Tom, because when you died—I mean when I thought you were dead—I was devastated that this would be something I could never make right. And I was sick with guilt about that.

"I was afraid, too, that the whole thing would come out if I was nominated to take your place as CEO, and due diligence would find what would look like embezzlement."

Winston leaned forward with his elbows on the arms of the chair and put his head in his hands.

The silence between the two men was deafening, the distinctive call of a loon out on the lake the only sound.

Chapter 60

DEREK AND TOM—SEPTEMBER 14

Derek had his phone in his pocket and earbuds in when the call came through. There was no time to waste.

He stood up and said, "Hey, Tom, sorry to interrupt, but you're needed up at the cottage right away."

"Excuse me, Winston, I'll be right back," Tom said as he responded quickly to Derek's instruction.

Derek told Tom to move fast, and as they climbed the stone steps leading to the cottage, Derek followed one step behind Tom, keeping his body between Tom and line of sight to Winston while speaking with the caller. When they entered the cottage, Derek hit the lock sequence on the security system and confirmed that Tom was safe.

"What's going on?" Tom asked.

Derek moved Tom away from the expansive front windows and explained that Detective Liu was on the line. Liu's first warrant to obtain financial records had unearthed large transactions within Winston's personal accounts in recent months that raised suspicion about the killer-for-hire theory.

Winston had bank accounts in Canada, the United States, and the Bahamas, which had attracted Liu's attention. Added to that was Elise's report of having overheard Winston's suspicious conversations at the office. And Winston's request for an in-person meeting with Tom had raised a big red flag for Liu.

Derek put Liu on speaker just as he was confirming with Derek whether he had checked Winston for a weapon when he arrived.

Tom said, "Hi, Jason. I think there may be a logical explanation for the transactions you're looking at. First, Winston bought a condo this summer, so you might see some money transfers related to that.

"And then there was a personal loan from Pellucid to Winston for a hundred thousand dollars that went back out of his account for a stock buy. Plus, you may see regular payments to an Atlanta bank where his family lives. Does that all track with what you're seeing?" Tom said.

Tom and Derek waited several minutes while Liu sifted through the account information.

"Yes, that looks like it lines up," Liu said. "Does everything seem normal with him, Tom?"

"Yes, there's nothing that strikes me as out of the ordinary," Tom said.

"Okay, good. Aside from the safety issue, Tom, is there something I should be following up on regarding misappropriation of company funds?" Liu asked astutely.

"No, all fine, thanks. This is something internal to Pellucid that I'll deal with," Tom replied.

"If you say so," Liu said. "Sorry for the false alarm, guys. Stay sharp though, Derek."

"For sure. We'll be in touch," Derek responded, putting the safety back on the semiautomatic pistol he kept loaded.

Chapter 61:

TOM AND WINSTON—SEPTEMBER 14

Tom decided that his CFO going rogue plus the prospect of another attack warranted something stronger than coffee. Before heading back down to resume his meeting with Winston, Tom grabbed a tray and gathered up a bottle of Scotch, a decanter of water, a couple of snifters, and some ice.

When he reached the terrace, Tom set the tray on the serving table and turned to Winston, who still looked distraught.

"Sorry for the interruption, Winston. And look, this is not an ideal scenario by any means," Tom said. "I don't need to tell you, of all people, that an officer in a company should never use business accounts as a personal ATM. And when that officer is the CFO, that's orders of magnitude worse. This would, of course, typically be cause for termination."

Winston nodded miserably and acknowledged the truth of Tom's comment.

"That said, this is not the end of the world. When I was supposedly dead, I had a lot of time at the safe house to think about what's important in life and about second chances," Tom said, as he sat back down in his chair.

"I appreciate that you brought this to my attention rather than trying to juggle the books and cover it up, which you could have done as CFO. I can see that this was a misjudgment that isn't characteristic of you.

"And we have all made mistakes. I bought a hefty amount of BlackBerry stock in its heyday and watched it all drain down the sewer in increments when they crashed. That was a big learning experience, and I came to appreciate the concept of diversification from that mess," Tom said.

"Thanks for that, Tom," Winston said.

Tom nodded and continued.

"So, here's what I would propose doing. Since I'm not actually dead, I still have all my assets," Tom said. "I will personally lend you the seventy thousand, so with that, along with selling thirty thousand in stock, you can repay Pellucid immediately. Show the out and in of funds on the books as a temporary expenditure of some kind that will wash with the auditors," Tom said. "You probably know the right way to do this better than me."

Winston gave Tom a look of amazement, seemingly astounded that Tom was going to help him make the situation whole.

"I've decided to support the acquisition and I'm confident that pretty soon, you'll have a nice payday from Crystal Clere," Tom added. "You can wipe out the personal debt to me when you have your share of the sale," Tom said.

"And don't panic if it doesn't go through. There will be other offers, so if not this one, then the next. There's no rush to pay me back."

Winston was silent, apparently humbled at Tom's generosity. He swallowed hard a couple of times and then told Tom that he wouldn't regret keeping him on and that he would forever owe Tom a debt of gratitude.

"Oh, don't think you get off Scot-Free, Winston Wilson," Tom admonished. "You have to promise you'll resist the temptation to do anything with 'borrowed money' ever again, no matter what. If there's a next time you're in a pinch, you'll come to me."

"For sure," Winston said. "And I guess I'm not getting the Porsche, right?"

"Ha! Nope, sorry, all bequests are off," Tom said with a laugh. "But you'll be able to pick your own ride someday soon, I'm sure of it!"

"That would be something," Winston said, finally looking much less stressed.

"By the way, when you get that acquisition money, you're paying for all the Scotch. And I mean *all* the Scotch. Speaking of which, let's have a real drink. I think we could both use one," Tom said.

"You might need that to be a double," Winston said.

"There's more?" Tom said incredulously.

"I'm afraid so," Winston said quietly.

Chapter 62:

WINSTON AND TOM—SEPTEMBER 14

As Derek kept a watchful eye from a few feet away, Tom poured generous shots of Scotch into the snifters with water on the side, and perched on the edge of his chair, clearly anxious to hear Winston's next revelation.

"Well, just before the attack on you, our software developers were reviewing a report from the beta test team in Raleigh, and they found some anomalies that they brought to my attention," Winston said.

"I've been wishing I had discussed it with you right away, but I wanted to be sure of all the facts before putting it on the table. And then you went and died," Winston said with a smile.

"How inconsiderate of me!" Tom joked. "So did you get to the bottom of it?"

"Yes, and you're not going to like this. As you're aware, James was supposed to be using the software to enable better analysis of buying patterns for use in social media. You know, specific retargeting so if you've been searching for a new vehicle, you suddenly start seeing ads in your social feed from local dealerships."

"Yes, leveraging the usual social media algorithms. So, what's the concerning part?" Tom asked.

"His company wasn't just using the software to boost e-commerce purchases. James and his Republican friends have been using it to figure out how to manipulate voting districts in North Carolina. It's called gerrymandering, and if they are stretching the scope to benefit their party, some legitimate voters could be disenfranchised as a result," Winston said.

"What?" Tom exclaimed so emphatically that Derek jumped. "You've got to be kidding! That is exactly the kind of abuse of technology I'm dead set against."

"I know," Winston said, nodding. "When I asked the development team why there were two distinct projects, only one of which was being used as the basis for a Pellucid case study, they said it was because there's a second layer of beta trialing going on. And that second layer was the political stuff.

"I took it up with James, and he implied that you were aware of it, but that didn't seem possible," Winston added.

"You've got that right! So James is using our software for a self-serving application for the benefit of him and his political cronies?" Tom said.

"Yes. From what I've found so far, James is analyzing voter patterns by neighborhood so that based on incredibly detailed data—surfaced in part by our software—North Carolina Republicans can restructure voting boundaries throughout the state to favor their party," Winston said. "When it's misused, gerrymandering is pretty devious."

Tom was aware that, since former President Trump's defeat and some unexpected results in swing states, many Republican leaders had demonstrated that they were willing to do literally anything to regain or maintain power. Georgia and Texas, among other states, had openly attempted to manipulate voting, putting forward legislation aimed at disenfranchising groups of voters known to support Democrats. Tactics in some states ranged from taking away polling stations, restricting mail-in voting, even legislating against bringing food and water to people waiting in line to vote—anything and everything to disenfranchise or discourage legitimate but non-Republican American voters.

Winston explained that redistricting amped up with gerrymandering can be a powerful tool, and sadly the people being disadvantaged by it are often nonwhite or low-income. Tom wanted no affiliation with this potentially undemocratic activity that his father-in-law was involved with in North Carolina.

"Winston, this is not a small problem," Tom said. "Crystal Clere is going to want to have access to all the beta trial data as a demonstration of how well Pellucid's software is performing. Is there any way we can ensure this Republican gerrymandering nonsense won't be part of that?" Tom asked.

"Yes, the good news is that our developers say there is enough legitimate data performance from standard practices that we can demonstrate viability without needing to share the other data-mining results," Winston said.

Tom exhaled. "Well, that's a relief. And as of now, the use of our software in North Carolina stops—and I'll tell James so myself!" Tom said, putting his glass down on the arm of the chair more forcefully than intended.

"I'm sorry for all the bad news today, Tom," Winston said sincerely.

"I appreciate that, Winston. But, I mean, at least you had the guts to tell me about your mistake and make things right. That's more than I can say for James. Or my wife—or my brother for that matter," Tom said.

"Come to think of it, things haven't been great since I came back to life," Tom added wryly.

"I'll ask Elise to research some background on gerrymandering so I can be fully prepared for the conversation with James. Set up a Zoom call for the three of us tomorrow, Winston, and we'll walk through all this in detail," Tom continued, determinedly. "And then I'll tackle my father-in-law."

Chapter 63:

LAWRENCE, TOM, AND WINSTON—
SEPTEMBER 14

Lawrence had been working at the cottage but was due to take a float plane back to Toronto in the afternoon for an in-studio media interview. He and Elise had just been on the phone figuring out several different ways for Lawrence to block questions about Tom and bridge to other things he wanted to discuss in the interview. It was inevitable that he would be asked about Tom since reporters knew Lawrence was an investor and board member at Pellucid.

Best to be fully prepared, Lawrence thought.

He saw Tom and Winston coming up the walkway to the cottage and decided to join them for lunch. Winston looked like a new man, obviously comfortable and talkative, which was a sea change from the last time Lawrence had seen him. It was good to have things returning to relative normal.

When their meal of squash soup followed by pan-fried rainbow trout and rice pilaf was completed, Tom confided in Lawrence about his father-in-law's misuse of Pellucid technology and the fact that he would be pulling the plug on access to the software. Tom also planned to share the situation with the board at their upcoming meeting, and James would no doubt be removed from the board as a result.

Lawrence took a few minutes on his own with a flavorful cigar outside on the main deck to consider this news.

Gerrymandering will certainly damage the Pellucid brand if it ever comes to light publicly. Tom is right that he needs to shut that down unequivocally and immediately, Lawrence thought.

Lawrence had known that something was up with James beyond the typical pros and cons assessment of an acquisition offer. *That man is infuriating, to say the least*, Lawrence thought. *No doubt James deliberately kept this from Tom, although he must have known it would come out sooner or later.*

Tom needed to put as much space as possible between himself and his father-in-law. And that was going to strain an already stressed marriage.

What a mess—but it's survivable for the business, Lawrence thought.

The Big Guy returned to the dining room to resume his discussion with Tom and Winston.

"Well, I agree with you, Tom, that work with James's company needs to be shut down right away," said Lawrence. "And I know dealing with this isn't easy for you, what with James being Miriam's father. But the damage from being associated with James and this underhanded, undemocratic activity could tank Pellucid's future."

Tom nodded in agreement. "Winston has pulled together a dossier of all the data-mining activity that James has undertaken, and once we've reviewed that tomorrow along with a report from Elise on gerrymandering, I'll call James and put an end to this," Tom said.

"Unfortunately, there's one other aspect of this situation I would suggest you deal with right away. As part of the due diligence exercise, the full use of the software needs to be disclosed to Crystal Clere, Tom," Lawrence said. "Otherwise, if and when it comes to light after they purchase the company, they would have recourse to renege on the deal. You're welcome to check with your lawyer, but I've seen this type of situation before, and it's best to address it head-on."

"Well, that's not good. I had hoped this would be something we could resolve before the acquisition and not have to reveal to Crystal Clere," Tom said, absorbing the full extent of Lawrence's counsel.

Lawrence reminded Tom of the Cambridge Analytica and Facebook scandal that unfolded in 2018, when data harvested from millions of Facebook users was exploited for political purposes in the 2016 US presidential election. Online privacy and data manipulation made major headline news, especially in the United States and the United Kingdom, and no company would want to repeat that debacle, Lawrence stressed.

"Yes, that would be a nightmare," Tom agreed. "I'll table the issue with Crystal Clere's CEO as soon as I quash the activity with James."

"If their CEO realizes that you dealt with the situation as soon as it came to your attention and that you plan to propose having James removed from the board ASAP, that should mitigate things," Lawrence said.

"I certainly hope so," Tom said.

"If I may, I have another suggestion for you."

"Of course," Tom said.

"It's important that Crystal Clere sees a united front from Pellucid, not splinter groups of warring tribes. Why don't we bring the key players up here on the weekend of the twenty-fifth for a discussion away from the office? We can hash out the pluses and minuses of selling the company and give everyone a chance to be heard. If we can get aligned on the acquisition, it will make the board meeting on the twenty-seventh less contentious," Lawrence said.

"Great idea, Lawrence. It's going to be uncomfortable no matter how we handle things after all the recent churn, but this could help," Tom agreed.

"That sounds like a good plan to me as well," Winston added.

"Okay, so the weekend off-site conference, we'll call it, will include you both, myself, Elise, Miriam, and James, and hopefully we can come to some understanding," Lawrence said. "Oh, and you too, Derek!" Lawrence said jokingly, musing that Derek had a talent for seeming invisible even though he was constantly present.

Lawrence was also thinking it would give him a chance to take James aside and threaten him within an inch of his life with public humiliation if he didn't step away from the board voluntarily—and meanwhile, support the acquisition. Tom didn't need to know all his motivations for the off-site, Lawrence thought.

Chapter 64:

ELISE—SEPTEMBER 15

Tom had sounded determined and angry when he called to tell Elise what James had been up to using Pellucid's software. She had honestly never heard of gerrymandering, so she was curious as she dove into Tom's request for a briefing package.

Her research showed that redistricting is a legitimate part of the American political system, whereby states redraw their legislative and congressional boundaries following the US census conducted every ten years. The primary intent is to balance voting districts based on population changes, referencing data collected in the census.

However, gerrymandering is a step beyond simple redistricting, whereby the redrawing of voting boundaries is deliberately manipulated for the benefit of a particular party, a process that can ultimately disenfranchise voters based on their political affiliation or ethnicity.

While in the past politicians had to rely on a lot of conjecture, now there is highly sophisticated technology like Pellucid's that enables refined data mining, similar to consumer goods searches and mapping software.

With advanced software, it's possible to map out neighborhoods and plug in census data about each household, and then overlay that with data about individual residents sourced from publicly available records such as drivers' licenses and gun permits.

Detail on individual voters also comes from information "mined" from data footprints—the telltale information we all leave scattered unknowingly and even carelessly across the internet—that anyone from research firms and marketers to political parties can access readily and cheaply.

So hyper targeted mapping using data mining and AI software makes it easy to figure out the impact of adjusting voting lines, Elise realized. *And neighborhoods with odd zigs and zags in their voting districts were probably gerrymandered at some point.*

Elise found that some reporting goes so far as to say that the computing ability of big data has revolutionized politics. She came across an interesting online *US News & World Report* article from July 2017 containing some key points she would pull out for Tom:

> ". . . as big data gets better at identifying voters, and their preferences, with near-surgical precision, gerrymandering . . . is only going to get worse."

> "While redistricting has always been a political scoundrel's art . . . the rise of big data has put gerrymandering on steroids."

What a great analogy, Elise thought. *Gerrymandering on steroids indeed!*

An August 22, 2021 article published by *The Guardian*'s online US site reported that the software most widely used for redistricting is Caliper Corporation's Maptitude.

According to the news report, this Boston-based company specializes in transportation software but customized its software for redistricting in the 1990s.

Commenting on extreme redistricting using their software, the head of Caliper told *The Guardian*, "We were horrified with what some people had done with our software. We were software guys, math guys. We were making tools and stuff. And we weren't invested in, you know, trying to make one side win against another or anything like that."

No wonder Tom is so incensed about Pellucid being involved in this, Elise thought. Pellucid was at risk of the same kind of negative implications thanks to James having hijacked beta tests underway in North Carolina.

She even found an article that referred to Republican gerrymandering as "Putin-style democracy."

Wow! Gerrymandering is contrary to all of Pellucid's core values, Elise noted. *And what a brand-image nightmare for Pellucid if the company became associated with the Republican Party's efforts in North Carolina! "Canadians helping subvert US democracy" would make quite a headline.*

Her research painted a complete picture of data analytics used in gerrymandering, and it wasn't pretty, Elise concluded. She sent Tom a summary report for review on the prep call with her and Winston, prior to his meeting with James.

Chapter 65:

TOM AND JAMES—SEPTEMBER 16

Tom and James were sizing each other up over Zoom. James had a stony expression and made only a marginal effort at pleasantries at the start of the call.

"James, thanks for being available to meet today," Tom said. His father-in-law nodded.

"I'll get right to the point here, so I make the best use of your time," Tom continued. "I'm calling a halt to the use of our software at your company. Your beta trial is wrapping up and the Pellucid case study is now completed, so we have everything we'll need to share with Crystal Clere. I appreciate the contribution that you've made to this point, but now we're done."

James looked genuinely taken aback and then angry.

"Now, why in the devil would you pull the plug on my company using Pellucid's software?" James said.

"Because our technology was not intended to be subverted for political purposes," Tom responded. He waited while that sunk in.

"What are you talking about?" James said.

"Let's not play games here, James. I have full transparency to the data you've been collecting and the purpose. Do I need to spell that out?"

"No," James said. "But you gave me the authority to oversee the beta trial and I chose to take the data mining in multiple directions. You don't need to go all high and mighty on me; this was the plan."

"We disagree on that point, James. I would never endorse the type of research that you've been doing nor use software analytics to suppress rightful voters," Tom said.

"Oh, because your Canadian system is so perfect, right? Your pretty-boy prime minister isn't getting great reviews lately. And apparently, Canadian police can't even be honest about someone not being dead," James scoffed.

"James, we've already established that we don't see eye to eye on a lot of things. Let's keep this to the issue at hand. The work is finished, and we're done with data analytics in North Carolina," Tom said.

"Fine. I hope that makes you and your girlfriend happy."

"Pardon me?" Tom said, not believing his ears.

"You heard me. Don't think I don't know the shameful way you've treated my daughter," James said.

"I think you're missing some of the facts, but I will not get into this with you, James. Have a good rest of the day," Tom said, closing the call before it dissolved into any further personal attacks.

Tom sat back and absorbed the depth of the rift with Miriam's father. It was apparent that if James accepted Lawrence's invitation to come to the cottage for the weekend, it would be a challenging and controversial time.

Chapter 66:

MIRIAM—SEPTEMBER 17

*T*he Four Seasons Hotel is at least a comfortable place for a person to hide out, Miriam thought as she looked out her window to the Yorkville neighborhood below, cradling a glass of Baco Noir wine in her hands.

She had been keeping a low profile, taking advantage of the on-site spa, and having delicious meals delivered to her room.

I deserve the pampering after all I've been through, Miriam told herself. *In what universe does someone's husband pretend to be dead and leave his wife completely out of the picture?*

And I'm not stupid enough to buy this nonsense of "the police said I couldn't tell you." It was no doubt that damn Detective Liu who put Tom up to this! Miriam fumed.

Miriam had always suspected from their very first meeting that Liu had never liked her, so it wasn't a stretch to conclude this was his doing.

Imagine Tom going along with such a plan and subjecting her to all this! Miriam thought indignantly. *And there's nothing like watching a pile of money dissipate into thin air because your husband is not, in fact, dead,* Miriam thought.

I hate to be cynical, but I would have been set for life! Now, I have the prospect of my marriage ending and getting less than half of the assets that would have been all mine. Patrick and I both were better off when Tom was dead. Sad but true, Miriam thought, gesturing on ironic "cheers" to this latest twist of fate as she turned and caught her reflection in the dresser mirror.

Meanwhile, Tom will ride off into the sunset on that damn horse with Elise, Miriam thought angrily. *Why should he be happy after causing all this chaos?*

Even more infuriating, Miriam was convinced that Elise had probably known all along about Tom being alive at the safe house.

And Miriam was absolutely mortified that she had held a memorial service for someone who was still alive.

How can I face my clients who will have seen everything play out in real time on social media and splashed all over the news? What a complete nightmare! Miriam refilled her wine-glass and contemplated her next steps.

This isn't over by a long shot. Tom is going to pay for what he did to me and for ruining our marriage! she thought determinedly.

Next weekend at Lawrence's would be her chance to confront a few people, including Elise, Miriam told herself.

Especially Elise.

 *Chapter 67:*

PATRICK—SEPTEMBER 17

With Tom resurfacing, the uncertainty around Pellucid's future, and his now precarious relationship with Miriam, everything felt a bit all over the map for Patrick. It was hard to concentrate on his new job at a start-up, which he didn't enjoy much anyway, so Patrick called in sick and planned to take a week off.

He had called Miriam to see if they could get together at her hotel, but she was worried about the optics of being with another man since her husband was still alive. So it certainly looked like their relationship was on hold.

Miriam told him Lawrence would be hosting the Pellucid executive team at his cottage next weekend.

Some kind of off-site Kumbaya session, no doubt. Everyone bonding around the campfire, Patrick thought disdainfully.

His master plan of Miriam inheriting all that lovely money and himself stepping in as the new man in her life had certainly crumbled when Tom showed up. On the bright side, Miriam would still get a whack of money and assets if they ended up divorcing. But it paled compared to the insurance and other payouts that would have happened if Tom were actually dead. And who knew what choices Miriam would make now?

Just my luck! Now there's no chance of returning to Pellucid either, Patrick realized. *That would be over Tom's dead body.*

Over Tom's dead body, Patrick repeated to himself.

Would I have the nerve to do something like that? Could I carry through if I had the chance to take Tom out of the picture once and for all? There would certainly be a lot to gain with Tom gone—for real this time.

That fool Detective Liu had questioned him about the purchase of the wire for the pen at the farm, so clearly he was considered a viable suspect. And the police had no doubt sullied his good name when checking out his alibis with his rugby mates, the barn manager, and worst of all the woman he had briefly dated in the summer.

She probably thinks I'm some kind of axe murderer! Patrick fumed. *And stupid city cop Liu hadn't known the difference between types of wire, or he wouldn't have been asking me about it in the first place!*

It was then that Patrick had a tempting thought.

If I'm being taken for a murderer, maybe I should live up to the accusation. . . . What the hell, maybe I'll go up north the weekend of the twenty-fifth to be close to the action!

Patrick wasted no time, making a reservation for two nights at a Port Severn inn and marina near Honey Harbour— and renting a boat.

 *Chapter 68:*

TOM—SEPTEMBER 22

What a crazy time it's been, Tom reflected as he sat on the balcony off his room at Lawrence's cottage.

On the positive side, he and Crystal Clere's CEO had a great discussion and things were looking good for the US $250 million acquisition—despite misuse of the software by James. So that was a relief.

Tom was not, however, looking forward to the upcoming weekend, which would be an entirely different scenario from his relatively peaceful time at the cottage. The off-site meeting would bring together all the key players, including Miriam and James, as everyone had accepted the invitation. Tom hoped interactions would remain civil in deference to Lawrence's hospitality, and that they would all find some common ground by the end of the weekend.

Tom decided at that moment it was time to move things forward on another much more positive front. He called Elise and invited her to join him in Caledon the next afternoon for a ride. Tom was anxious to spend time with Elise and reunite with Titan.

Derek wasn't happy about the idea but agreed that no one would be able to anticipate Tom showing up at the barn, so the risk level was minimal.

Tom asked the chef if he could pack a picnic lunch for them, and he was excited about getting back in the saddle. It would be well worth the two-hour drive each way to see the loves of his life.

 *Chapter 69:*

TOM, ELISE, DEREK, AND TITAN—SEPTEMBER 23

t's a gorgeous day, perfect for our ride, Elise thought as she pulled her SUV into the stable yard. Tom and Derek had already arrived, and Derek was working up enough courage to pat Titan over the gate to his field. Derek grew up in the city and had never encountered such a huge horse.

Tom was ecstatic to see Titan, and the bond between them was clear, Elise noted as she approached.

So many broken hearts are now healed with Tom back, Elise thought contentedly.

Tom saw Elise and rushed over to give her an enthusiastic hug and a kiss on the cheek.

After being cooped up for weeks, he's as excited as a schoolboy to be back at the barn, Elise thought, smiling.

By contrast, Derek looked worried and expressed concern that as a non-rider he would not be able to stay close to Tom if they left the outdoor riding ring near the barn. Elise pointed out that not only had their decision to come to Caledon been very last-minute, but she had picked a new route for them to explore today, so no one could anticipate their path.

Derek agreed that the risk was low but insisted on borrowing the barn's ATV so he could follow them at a distance that wouldn't spook the horses.

"Poor Derek, he isn't used to the people he's protecting going rogue," Tom joked to Elise after they mounted up and headed out on their ride.

"I know, he takes looking after you very seriously. But so do I," Elise said, smiling.

Tom and Elise rode side by side, with Titan towering over the more delicate Cadette as the horses walked along the edge of the field.

Deciding to dispense with work matters first, Elise shared with Tom that Nate seemed to have satisfied his urge for notoriety and it didn't appear that he had done any media interviews since the weekend. So there should be no fresh nuggets about Tom and Pellucid to feed the news cycle, at least for now.

Tom filled Elise in on what seemed like a permanent rift with Nate. And if his brother kept his word, family disclosures to the media would no longer be a concern.

Tom also shared that the discussion with James had been contentious and that he anticipated the upcoming weekend would be a challenge, and Elise agreed.

"Well, let's just put all that aside for now and enjoy the day," Tom said, moving Titan up into a trot. At one point, Cadette had to canter to keep up because Titan covered so much ground with his huge strides.

The air smelled delicious and fresh, and the countryside was starting to turn color for fall. Elise was glad to be off the main roads and in the fields because so many gawkers came out of the city at this time of year to admire Caledon's beauty.

This is my version of heaven, riding on a perfect day with a special person. No, make that with the special person that I love, Elise corrected herself.

Chapter 70

TOM AND ELISE—SEPTEMBER 23

Tom had always found Elise to be beautiful, but today she was simply stunning. With her blond hair streaming out behind her from under a riding helmet, her blue shirt billowing in the breeze, and an expression of complete joy on her face, Elise had never looked more lovely.

Tom had a lot to share with Elise and wasn't quite sure where to begin. At the safe house, he'd had enormous chunks of time to just think, compared with the frenetic pace of his normal life—which gave him ample opportunity to be more purposeful.

He had realized that burying his true feelings wasn't going to work. He had been ignoring the state of his marriage, making do with the situation, and pushing feelings of discontent aside. Now with Miriam having moved on with Patrick so quickly, there seemed no point in prolonging the relationship. It had run its course, and it was time to end things.

And, in fact, he was in love with Elise. He had always told himself that it would be normal for anyone to appreciate a smart, fun, beautiful person like Elise, but it was more than that. His heart skipped a beat whenever he saw her, her beauty took his breath away, they had the same thoughts and dreams and values, and she was his person.

It's time to recognize these truths and do something about them, and today is the day, Tom vowed.

Tom suggested to Elise that they stop to enjoy the view from a particularly striking vantage point. They dismounted and stood beside the horses, enjoying the panorama of fields bordered by crimson sumac bushes. Derek was behind them on the trail, doing his best to be discreet.

"Elise, I suggested riding today for two reasons. I admit one was to see my boy Titan."

Elise laughed and nodded.

"The other is I desperately needed to see you. I need to tell you that I love you."

Elise looked surprised but delighted and said, "Well, the truth is, I've always loved you, Tom. But I think you know that."

"I had hoped, of course," Tom said. "I know I'm not in a position to offer anything at this point, but I have decided to get a divorce. There's no way forward for Miriam and me, and I think that was the case well before the attack happened."

"Oh, I'm sorry, Tom," Elise said.

"You are?" Tom said with exaggerated drama, teasing.

"Well, not sorry that you will be a free man, but sorry for your loss," Elise said. "Because I know that you and Miriam were together a long time, and no matter what, saying goodbye to a chapter in your life isn't easy."

"It will be a tough go until this is all resolved. And I don't wish anything but good things for Miriam," Tom said. "But I do want to move forward. With you."

"I'll be ready to move forward too, whenever the time is right," Elise said.

Suddenly Tom winced and rubbed his neck.

"Tom, are you alright?" Elise asked, looking worried that riding today might have been too much for him.

"Um, my neck has a knot in it. Maybe you can help?" Tom suggested, as Elise slipped around in front of Cadette and felt the back of Tom's neck.

Tom surprised her by smiling as he ran his hand along the edge of her face and retrieved a piece of hay that was embedded in her hair.

"Actually, I'm feeling just fine now that I'm next to you," Tom said as he put his hand on the small of her back, pulling Elise close to him. And after a moment when their eyes connected, he kissed her.

Elise kissed Tom back until Titan gave his owner a shove with his nose and made them both laugh. And as they kissed again, Tom knew this was the beginning of a new phase in their relationship. And he hoped Elise would always look at him with the same adoration in her eyes that he cherished today.

When they were back at the stable, they opened the picnic basket and set out the delicious contents on a table near the paddocks. Tom said it couldn't be a more ideal day, but Derek expressed the opinion that their picnic was a little too close to smelly farm animals, especially the potbellied pig!

 *Chapter 71:*

PATRICK—SEPTEMBER 23

After more time on his own at home, Patrick realized he had surprised himself when—just for a fleeting moment—he had considered the possibility of killing Tom.

As he lathered up and shaved off a couple of days' growth, he questioned how that could have even crossed his mind. *Ridiculous!*

He hadn't meant it, but it was still a terrible thought. It was at that moment when Patrick had a bit of an epiphany about just how desperate he was to recover what he'd had at Pellucid and to exact revenge.

Not an attractive thing to admit about myself, he told his reflection in the mirror.

Patrick thought about what his father had said about being fired. When it happened, his dad had told him it would take a while to adjust after pouring so much of his effort and identity into Pellucid with Tom. And Patrick now realized he had been right—it had been a harder blow than he had admitted to himself at the time.

His poor dad had listened to lots of venting ever since, and lately, Patrick had gone on about the nerve of Tom Oliver to have reappeared, ruining his prospects with Pellucid and possibly Miriam too.

And the man had heard enough. His father had called from Ireland a couple of days ago and put Patrick in his place.

"Pat, you've been feeling sorry for yourself and, I might add, behaving rather shamefully," his father said. "Everyone has setbacks in life, but it's how we deal with those bad things that defines what kind of man we are.

"You know that throughout my life, things haven't always been clear sailing either," Patrick's dad continued. "But I've always believed what my hero Frank Sinatra once said: the best revenge is massive success. You don't need to go looking for other kinds of revenge.

"You're still young—for heaven's sake you're only thirty-seven years old—you've got some good severance money in your bank account, you've got the smarts, and all you need to do is smarten up and get on with it!" he said emphatically. "There's no reason on God's green earth that you can't decide what you want to do next and have massive success. You don't need Tom or Pellucid or any of those people to be amazing in your own right."

Patrick hadn't enjoyed being called out, but he knew it was all true. He had been on a slow boil ever since the firing and was spending his time thinking about how to take money and power back from Tom. When his dad spelled it out like that, it sounded petty.

He had to admit to himself that he had behaved like an ass and paid the consequences, and it was on him, Patrick McGowan, and no one else. And that was hard to acknowledge.

His father also suggested making amends with the Pellucid team and leaving things on better terms.

"You never know who you'll end up working for or who will end up working for you in the long run, so be careful what bridges you burn in business," his dad had said.

It won't be easy putting this all behind me, Patrick thought. *But maybe Dad is right that moving on with a bit of dignity would be a better way forward.*

Patrick decided that—hard as it would be—he would attempt to mend fences.

Since Patrick had already booked the weekend in Port Severn near Lawrence's cottage, he would go to the cottage on Saturday to extend the proverbial olive branch.

It might kill him to be humble, but he would try his best. Before leaving Toronto, he would buy some flowers for Miriam, Elise, and Grace and pick up some well-aged Scotch and good cigars for the men. It was time to move on.

Chapter 72:

DETECTIVE LIU—SEPTEMBER 23

When Tom updated him on the plan for the weekend, Liu was not pleased. The whole idea of having Tom at the cottage was the remoteness of the place and the intent to keep him safe. Now the foxes had been invited into the henhouse, what with all the key Pellucid players attending.

In a way, it reminded Liu of COVID because the longer the pandemic was around, the less vigilant everyone seemed about prevention. It seems to be human nature that the more time we live with a bad situation, the more normalized it becomes. In this case, however, even if all seems normal, there could be a third attempt on Tom's life. And that threat had not diminished.

Liu decided it was best for him to plan to spend the weekend at the cottage as reinforcement for Derek, and Lawrence had kindly accommodated him. The OPP marine unit that patrols that area of Georgian Bay would pick Liu up in Honey Harbour, take him to the cottage, and be available for backup if needed.

Liu always found it interesting that the OPP managed the local waters and the Canadian Coast Guard had jurisdiction in the deeper waters away from the channels. Few people realize that Georgian Bay is a huge body of water, about 80 percent the size of Lake Ontario and covering something like 5,800 square miles.

Those marine OPP officers have the best job, Liu thought, *mostly patrolling the waters in powerful cabin cruisers, looking for boaters consuming alcohol or engaged in other infractions.*

Well, here we go, Liu thought. *Another opportunity to see some of the key players in action. And Tom had been raving about Lawrence's chef, so that wouldn't be hard to take.*

 *Chapter 73:*

LAWRENCE—SEPTEMBER 24

awrence was aware that he was preparing for one of his most challenging conciliation meetings ever, to help the Pellucid core team air perspectives and hopefully get on board for the acquisition. Everyone invited to attend had accepted his offer to come for the weekend. He needed to review the logistics.

Tom and Derek were back from Caledon, so they were already at the cottage. Check.

Elise would be arriving tonight, and Lawrence would pop over in the runabout and pick her up at the Honey Harbour town dock. Check.

Detective Liu had decided to join them out of an abundance of caution. The OPP would pick him up tomorrow morning in their patrol boat in advance of everyone else arriving. Check.

Winston would be driving up from Toronto in the morning and a water taxi would meet him at the town dock. Check.

James was planning to fly his plane to the downtown Toronto Island airport tonight and had rented a float plane to fly himself and Miriam up to the cottage in the morning. He had done that once before, so Lawrence had no concerns about him finding the island. Check and check.

Lawrence's chef had some great meals planned. A selection of wines from Italy, California, and Ontario had been brought in. And the bar had been restocked with premium Scotch and some whiskey from a Collingwood, Ontario, distillery that Lawrence was considering investing in. With any luck, the scenery, accommodations, and top-shelf food and drink would set the right tone for an amicable weekend. *Fingers crossed,* Lawrence thought.

PART FOUR

Chapter 74:

JAMES—SEPTEMBER 24

Angry didn't adequately describe how James was feeling when he finished the call with Tom about shutting down data mining at his company using Pellucid software. He was downright incandescent with rage. James spoke with Miriam and found that she was still equally infuriated with Tom, and he felt justified in all his actions.

When James had realized a few months ago that Tom might sell Pellucid and take away the means needed to collect and leverage voter data for the Republican Party, he had known something had to be done. James had every intention of gaining more control, not less, of Pellucid's software research and development. After all, he had worked on voting districts in only two cities so far. There was much more work to be done to ensure the success of his party in North Carolina and beyond.

James had hoped to eventually mold Tom into someone who could work with him to create a more perfect political system, but that was not going to happen. And there was no room in his world for a namby-pamby liberal like Tom.

Added to the business issues was the breakdown of Tom and Miriam's marriage, swirling into a perfect storm in his mind.

Imagine a potential divorce in our family after such a high-society wedding! Miriam would have much better social standing as a widow than a divorcee, James thought. *I was absolutely justified in doing what I had to do: plan Tom's demise in the interest of the greater good and to protect my daughter.*

With Tom out of the picture, James would have been able to justify the Republican data research with the help of his hand-picked CEO replacement and move forward with his objectives. But now with Tom back, all his goals were in jeopardy.

There's no doubt in my mind that Sarge is needed again, James thought.

Sarge was just the man to remove Tom from the equation once and for all, and James had hired him to take action. James and Sarge had been good friends ever since the old days when they were both in the National Guard. Sarge was now a follower of QAnon and had been sharing their ideas with James. Neither James nor Sarge needed convincing to firmly believe that Trump had been cheated out of reelection and that their support was needed to restore the country to glory.

Sarge had been part of the January 6 Capitol insurrection. James wasn't sure of Sarge's role, and it was probably better that he didn't know too many details, but he was incredibly proud of Sarge for being there.

And Sarge was loyal to James and supported his political ambitions, hoping that someday the Republican Party would take over the government once and for all. They both agreed that it was time for a revolution. To hell with the two-party system. Forget democracy. This would be a Republican world with Trump as emperor or whatever he wanted to call himself. Just like Trump's hero Putin. Sarge was all-in for making it happen when James had told him this needed to be done for the benefit of all.

Even better, Sarge knew Toronto well because he had spent summers visiting relatives there and had even vacationed at his aunt's cottage on Georgian Bay. *Who could be a better fit?* James thought.

Sarge had apologized to James that he had not succeeded in running Tom down in Yorkville. There had been too many potential witnesses around, so he had aborted the attempt at the last minute.

And when James called Sarge to tell him Tom had reappeared after the Caledon attack, Sarge could scarcely believe it. He had been sure Tom was a goner when he left him for dead on the rocks.

Sarge had told James he was committed to making damn sure the third time he would be successful. "Stand back and stand by," Trump told the Proud Boys prior to January 6—and Sarge had been standing by too, already in Canada and waiting for James to give the word.

For his part, James was getting his plane prepped today and would be heading north soon for the off-site meeting. James was pleased that this would soon be over, once and for all, and everything would be as it should—just as his two masters, the Lord and Donald Trump, would want.

 *Chapter 75:*

SARGE—SEPTEMBER 24

I t was early evening, and Sarge sat in the screened-in porch of the cabin he had rented on an island just north of Lawrence Cameron's enclave, thinking about his upcoming final assignment. The limited opportunity to get to Tom during the Pellucid offsite meeting would make this a challenge. Plus, James had given him the heads-up that Tom had a security guy.

I'll have to be quick and decisive to get the bastard, Sarge thought.

Sarge had rented a top-of-the-line speedboat for the job. He did some practice runs earlier in the day, and the boat handled like a dream. And Sarge was well prepared to navigate the challenging waters—full of hidden rocky outcroppings and tricky shoals—having boated here while visiting his aunt back in the day. Sarge was looking forward to getting this done and making good on the whack of cash James had already paid him after the attack in Caledon.

Sarge had taken on this kind of assignment before, but only for people who had legitimate reasons for needing someone gone. And they had to be dedicated evangelicals and committed to a revolution in America. Sarge had his principles and, as such, did not consider himself a hired gun.

He and James were like-minded and had kept in touch for the thirty years since they both served in the National Guard. It had been a great training ground for them, and they'd learned about weapons handling and combat strategies. Ironically, in the Guard, they had been called up at the direction of the president at the time to settle civil unrest situations.

They had both found their philosophy diverging from the rank-and-file mainstream thinking of the state and federal legislative hypocrites who called the shots, and they left the Guard after five years. But they were proud of their service.

However, the proudest and most exhilarating day of Sarge's life was January 6, 2021: the day he and his fellow patriots stormed the US Capitol.

No one knew exactly how things were going to play out that day, but they were planning to do everything they could to "Stop the Steal" and prevent the certification of the presidential election. Adrenaline pumped through his veins as they marched on the Capitol building, and he saw the QAnon Shaman leading others inside. Sarge remained outside to help erect a scaffold and started the chant, "Hang Mike Pence!"

Sarge would have liked Trump to have kept his promise to march with them, but he was happy to hear afterward that Trump had watched everything unfold on TV. And by all accounts, the president had enjoyed every minute of the chaos and carnage—and had done nothing to stop it. They were Trump's foot soldiers, and Sarge had not let their leader down.

The rest is history, as they say, Sarge reflected. Some of the people he knew had been interviewed by the FBI afterward, and two had been arrested. Thus far, Sarge had made it under the radar screen, so his travel hadn't been restricted. He had been lucky enough not to be caught on video at the event and cagey enough not to comment on social media, unlike others who had been sufficiently reckless to brag to the media about their role that day. Sarge couldn't blame them for being proud, though.

Ha, guess that's what made some of them Proud Boys, Sarge cackled to himself.

It rankled him that after the dust settled, many Republicans—including lawmakers who had been in the Capitol building during the insurrection—tried to downplay what happened on January 6. One of the idiots in Congress even said the insurrection was "no different from a regular tourist visit." What the hell was that guy thinking? Of course it was different!

It made no sense to Sarge why anyone would whitewash everything and pretend nothing major had happened. Doing so denied the message that QAnon followers, the Oath Keepers, Proud Boys, and everyone else had sent that day, loud and clear: that they would do anything to keep Trump in office.

And I mean anything! Sarge thought.

Memories of the insurrection had his blood pumping again, and Sarge planned to take that energy and focus it on killing Tom Oliver tomorrow. That would be a coup of a different kind to make things better for his friend James and for Republicans as a whole.

Sarge logged into the marine forecast for Saturday, and it was clear with a light wind. James had texted and said everything was a go. Sarge would do a final check of the boat before turning in tonight, ready for action in the morning.

 *Chapter 76:*

THE OFF-SITE MEETING—SEPTEMBER 25

Tom had a slight headache, but this time it was because of too much fun. Last evening, Lawrence had met Elise at the town dock as planned and brought her to the cottage. Tom and Elise had a great time having drinks and chatting with Lawrence and Grace—and of course with Derek included—gathered around the cozy outdoor fireplace until after midnight.

Oh well, it's nothing some extra-strength ibuprofen can't fix, Tom thought. He grabbed the meds and a mug of coffee before heading down to the dock with Derek to meet Winston.

The water taxi bringing Winston to the cottage pulled up earlier than scheduled. This time, Winston was prepared for Derek's inspection greeting. Once Winston had the all-clear, Tom and Derek walked him up to the first deck level where Elise was waiting and there was a midmorning spread of fruit, pastries, and coffee to enjoy. Winston noted that this would be an important day and wished Tom luck.

Detective Liu was due to arrive on the OPP boat any minute, so Tom and Derek walked back down to the deck. As a sleek speedboat raced by, Tom commented on what a nice design it was. The speedboat was circling at the end of the channel as the OPP's imposing cabin cruiser pulled up to the dock. Liu stepped off and waved to the two officers as they headed back toward Honey Harbour.

Timing was working out perfectly because the channel became clear of watercraft just as the float plane James piloted approached. James landed the plane mid-channel and steered it across the water to tie up. James and Miriam stepped out onto the dock, and James grabbed their overnight bags.

With Liu at his side and Derek also on the dock, Tom welcomed them and helped Miriam navigate the dock in precarious high-heeled shoes. As expected, Miriam and James were both polite but aloof.

"You remember my friend, Detective Jason Liu, I'm sure," Tom said. "He's here in an official capacity today."

Liu explained that he was leading the investigation into the attacks on Tom, which necessitated requiring James to show what was in his pockets and to unzip his leather duffle bag. James complied, and without being asked, Miriam opened her overnight bag and her sizable vintage Birkin handbag to show Liu the contents.

As they did the brief security check, James seemed jumpy, looking around as if to get the lay of the land. When Liu gave the nod, James suggested to Miriam that they take their things up to the cottage, and they walked up the stone steps together. Lawrence greeted them as he passed them on his way down to chat with Elise and Winston.

Tom couldn't resist a peek at the float plane, shielding his eyes from the sun so he could see the cockpit through the glass. Detective Liu, Derek, and Tom had just turned to join the others on the terrace when the speedboat swung back toward the cottage and veered closer.

Liu looked back and caught sight of a gun in the driver's right hand. He responded instantly, flattening Tom onto the dock and throwing himself on top as a bullet pierced the air just above them.

Derek positioned himself on the dock behind the float plane and shouted to Liu that he would provide cover. As the boat rapidly circled for another attempt, Liu yelled for everyone to get down, and he and Tom kept low to the ground as they moved for protection behind the stone retaining wall.

Sarge swung the speedboat by the dock and took a shot at Derek, who returned fire as the boat accelerated in another tight circle.

Liu had immediately contacted the OPP marine unit, and they turned their cruiser around and raced back up the channel with siren blaring. With the police on his tail, Sarge took off driving the speedboat as fast as he dared, skillfully weaving his way through the islands and aiming for the main channel that led to the open waters of Georgian Bay.

It would be only a few more minutes before Sarge could really open the motor up and possibly outrun the police. But the OPP had radioed the Coast Guard, and their large boat surged across the channel, cutting off Sarge's access.

Faced with five officers staring him down from the decks of two police boats, all with guns drawn, Sarge had no option but to surrender. The OPP took him into custody, with one of the Coast Guard crew now driving Sarge's speedboat and following the OPP cruiser back toward Honey Harbour. Both watercraft were now heading back up the channel leading to Lawrence's cottage.

Chapter 77:

JAMES—SEPTEMBER 25

When James and Miriam walked up to the top deck of the cottage, Grace greeted them and invited Miriam to get settled in her room. James said he would be in momentarily, and he watched the dock area from the cottage deck. He saw Sarge approaching at high speed and the shots fired, cursing another missed opportunity when Sarge took off with police in pursuit.

James had been having doubts about how successful an attack in broad daylight would be. But there weren't many options for Tom to be in a vulnerable location throughout the weekend. Now he regretted having listened to Sarge on timing.

James had his binoculars trained on the OPP cruiser and Sarge's speedboat as they both rounded a nearby island and continued back up the channel toward Lawrence's cottage. "Dammit," he muttered. James was distraught to see that Sarge was in handcuffs and the authorities had commandeered Sarge's boat.

James had no choice but to get out of Canadian jurisdiction as soon as possible, since the police would no doubt quickly connect him with Sarge. There was no time to spare.

He needed to get to the plane fast without attracting attention and would have to call Miriam later to explain.

James grabbed his overnight bag and hurried back down the stone steps, past the various seating areas, and down to the dock.

He saw Liu on the lower deck with the others and knew the detective would react. Sure enough, as James got to the dock and was untying the moorings, Liu was tailing him and yelling for him to stay on the island. James ignored him, jumping into the plane from the passenger side and sliding across into the pilot's seat. When Liu tried to open the passenger door, James pulled out a handgun that had been concealed under his seat, aiming it at the detective.

Liu held up his hands to indicate James was free to go.

That idiot probably thinks I'm going to change planes in Toronto, but I can fly this thing to the States, James thought. He had enough fuel to make it to the Thousand Islands area near Kingston, landing on the US side of Lake Ontario where he could ditch the plane and escape from there.

James started the engine and idled the plane into position in the channel. With police coming up the channel fast, he needed to get airborne quickly. He throttled up the aircraft and started accelerating across the water.

James had little time to react when a random powerboat suddenly cut across his takeoff path. He pulled up just in time to avoid a collision. But he had overcorrected and was struggling for control. He thought of his beautiful daughter as the cliff loomed in front of him.

 *Chapter 78:*

DETECTIVE LIU—SEPTEMBER 25

O PP who had Sarge in custody called Liu to say they had apprehended the shooter, advising that Liu needed to lock down the scene quickly while they arranged to bring an investigative team to the island. When Liu tried to prevent James from leaving and the gun was pulled, Liu had his answer as to whether any of Tom's inner circle were involved in the murder attempts.

As the plane taxied away from the dock, Liu contacted the OPP officers to warn them that James was entering the channel and was armed. Liu advised it was best to let James take off and law enforcement would deal with him wherever he landed.

Liu watched as the float plane accelerated across the water and was shocked when it veered off course to avoid a fast-moving powerboat that seemed to appear out of nowhere.

He was in disbelief as, within a matter of seconds, the plane crashed spectacularly into the cliff opposite Lawrence's cottage, causing a massive, fiery explosion.

The plane's fractured fuselage strafed down the cliff, fire hissing as it hit the water, with clouds of smoke and steam billowing up.

Following the deafening explosion, Liu looked back at the cottage and saw Miriam standing at the rail of the top deck, where she must have immediately absorbed the reality of what had happened. The sound of her mournful scream— like something from a wounded animal—pierced the air and ricocheted off the nearby rocks as she witnessed the certainty of her father's death.

Liu saw her take off her high heels and dash down the steps to the terrace, where Tom grabbed her and gently restrained her. Miriam was hysterical, sobbing that she wanted to go to her father, but there was nothing to be done.

Shards of the plane cascaded into the channel and paper-thin charred bits blew onto Lawrence's dock and onto the deck of the now stationary boat that had almost collided with the plane.

It was as if a bomb had gone off. And when Liu again turned and looked up from the dock, he could see Grace on the upper deck and everyone else standing on the lower terrace, all immobile as if frozen in time—while James P. Robinson Jr.'s life and his grandiose ambitions dissipated in the dark waters of Georgian Bay.

Chapter 79:

PATRICK—SEPTEMBER 25

Patrick had spent a quiet Friday night at the inn, enjoying a delicious steak dinner as he looked out on the water from the inn's atrium dining room. Now, on Saturday morning, he was up early and planning to arrive at Lawrence's cottage before everyone got embroiled in Pellucid business.

Feeling optimistic about making amends, he parked at the Honey Harbour marina and picked up the keys to his rented boat—a Hurricane 185 sporty-style bowrider with max 115 horsepower. *That will do nicely*, he thought.

He loaded the flowers and gifts and set out for the cottage, which was an easy route from the marina if he followed the marked channel.

Lawrence's cottage was located past the mouth of the inland waterway where the channel widened. Patrick decided to put the boat's engine to the test and throttled it up as he rounded the end of a neighboring island. The boat shot forward with impressive acceleration. And it was only then that Patrick saw a float plane taxiing across the water, traveling at high speed and headed straight for him.

It seemed too late to avoid a crash, so Patrick swerved to prevent colliding head-on. The plane took off at the last possible moment, narrowly missing the prow of his boat. But instead of continuing in line with the channel, the plane veered off-course and careened into the rocky outcropping directly across the water from Lawrence's cottage.

The explosion seemed to suck in the atmosphere and spit out ruin, as pieces of debris rained down, landing on Patrick's boat and in the water all around it.

Patrick stopped the boat amid the clouds of smoke and steam. The air was so dense with fumes it made his eyes water and his throat burn.

When the smoke began to clear, Patrick saw an OPP cruiser and a speedboat converging on Lawrence's cottage, and another OPP boat fast approaching from the direction of Honey Harbour. Patrick was surprised to see Detective Liu standing on Lawrence's dock, signaling that Patrick should pull his boat in.

It was only after docking and speaking with the detective that Patrick realized the magnitude of what had happened, and that it had been James flying the plane.

 *Chapter 80:*

LAWRENCE—SEPTEMBER 25

awrence had known that the off-site meeting would be
challenging, but this was well beyond anything he could
have imagined. It was Saturday night, and things had finally
settled down after such a shocking day. Lawrence was taking a
moment on the upper deck by himself to collect his thoughts.

All their guests had been interviewed by police and
given statements, and some had opted to return home after
the tragedy. Patrick had left earlier, and Winston had offered
to drive Miriam back to Toronto that evening, so they were
now enroute to Toronto. Miriam, who was understandably
in shock, had been inconsolable all day despite Grace's best
efforts to comfort her.

Tom and Elise had chosen to stay with Lawrence and
Grace as they all tried to process everything that had happened. Liu and Derek were also staying over but had already
excused themselves for the night, no doubt exhausted after
such a day. Lawrence had invited them to stay longer, but Liu
needed to get back to Toronto in the morning to file his report
and said he would give Derek a ride back to the city.

Police had informed Tom that the shooter, an American,
had called James a hero who died in support of his country, his

faith, and QAnon. This "Sarge" character was unabashed in admitting—bragging, really—that he had been hired by James to kill Tom and that he was the perpetrator of the three attempts on Tom's life. He was disappointed that he had let down James, his friend and fellow patriot, by failing to eliminate Tom. And he was devastated that his friend was dead.

Police were glad not to listen to any more of his deranged political views when they dropped Sarge off with the Midland OPP detachment for processing. From there he would be transferred to Toronto.

The investigating team had scoured the island all day, recovering bullets, measuring trajectories, and taking statements. With multiple OPP cruisers tied up at the dock and the burned-out body of the plane partly submerged and resting against the rocky outcropping across the channel, their cottage had attracted curious boaters who had now dispersed.

Detective Liu's fellow officers had congratulated him after having narrowly prevented Tom from being shot. And Derek was credited too for providing cover while everyone got out of harm's way.

Lawrence was still astounded that it had been Patrick McGowan driving the boat that almost collided with James's plane. Patrick was the last person any of them would have expected to show up during the off-site. And the coincidence of timing was beyond surreal.

When the police interviewed Patrick, he said he had come to the cottage to make amends, something almost equally shocking. Lawrence shook his head thinking about it. With flowers and high-end Scotch on board Patrick's boat, it seemed credible that was what he intended. And Patrick did apologize to Tom before leaving, both for having blamed Tom for everything and for being an opportunist with Miriam and Pellucid.

Given Patrick's role in James's death, it seemed unlikely to Lawrence that Patrick and Miriam would have any future together. Lawrence suspected that was a rebound relationship anyway, with both Miriam and Patrick acting out, each in their own way, after becoming estranged from Tom. Lawrence's heart did go out to Miriam because now she had lost not only both her parents—but likely her relationship with her husband as well.

To make matters worse, how awful for Miriam that her father was responsible for the murder attempts on Tom, Lawrence thought.

And Miriam would have other challenges. Despite Sarge's confession, police were still investigating whether her father had any accomplices. Miriam was a person of interest in view of the information Detective Liu had unearthed showing how extensively Miriam would have benefited from Tom's death. Under the circumstances, she was told to keep Detective Liu apprised of her whereabouts when she returned to Toronto and not to leave the city.

As for Tom, he seemed to be coping with all that had happened, but Grace had cautioned Lawrence not to be too sure. The fact that your father-in-law was determined to have you murdered was no small thing. And the way James had died in an explosive crash was horrifying for everyone.

It will take some time for all of us to get past this, Lawrence thought.

On that note, Lawrence stepped back inside the cottage, where Grace and Elise were having sherry to calm their nerves and Tom was pouring a Scotch.

"Hey, quit hogging that Scotch and pour another one, young man. And there's a cigar out here on the deck with your name on it," Lawrence said.

He gave Tom a supportive pat on the shoulder as they moved out onto the deck. The two men sat looking at the stars reflected in the calmest of waters—a contrast to all the turmoil that had taken place that day.

 *Chapter 81:*

THE TORONTO STAR—NOVEMBER 3

Editor's note:

It unfolds like a Netflix whodunit, but in fact it's a true and riveting story of attempted murder, ambition, business, politics, and even love. It all came to a spectacular conclusion on September 25 at the private island cottage owned by investment mogul Lawrence Cameron. The fiery plane crash that ended the life of US businessman James P. Robinson Jr. followed the purported death in August of his son-in-law, Pellucid CEO Tom Oliver, and multiple attempts on Oliver's life. Oliver is the son of former Toronto chief of police, the late John Oliver.

Driven by what police have described as the desire for power and fueled with political and religious zeal, Robinson engaged a killer for hire to murder Tom Oliver. Robinson's misuse of Pellucid technology to skew upcoming elections in his home state of North Carolina had been discovered. And the realization that his only daughter, Miriam, might be divorced and disenfranchised from what he saw as her rightful place in her husband's life and his company added to Robinson's motivation for murder.

The story has ended with Tom Oliver, still alive despite those targeted attempts on his life, championing the sale of Pellucid to California artificial intelligence company Crystal Clere Solutions for US $300 million. The price tag was even higher than anticipated because of competitive bids for Pellucid, which had gained increased brand visibility and popularity in the aftermath of the murder attempts.

In the first of a three-part series, senior writer Dan Reynolds will chronicle this colorful story as seen through the eyes of the lead investigator, Toronto Police Services Detective Jason Liu.

Detective Liu was challenged to untangle a complex set of circumstances and motivations to resolve the case. And had it not been for the heroic actions of the detective, along with OPP officers from multiple detachments and the Coast Guard, the outcome could have been quite different.

Here is part one of our series, "Devious Web."

EPILOGUE

Elise was relaxing on a chaise lounge beside the pool at their estancia about two hours' drive from Buenos Aires, Argentina. She and Tom had finally finished all the ins and outs of the Pellucid acquisition, and before moving to California to fulfill their two-year commitment to work as part of Crystal Clere's team, they had taken a much-needed vacation. They had both wanted to see Argentina's famous Pampas horse country someday, so this was a big bucket-list item fulfilled.

Their estancia, Spanish for "ranch," was one of many in the plains area of Argentina where horse sports and working horses abounded—including everything from polo training centers to cattle ranching. The local horses were mostly descended from Spanish horses brought to South America during the founding of Buenos Aires. They were hardy horses, considered to have exceptional endurance, and they would be fun to ride if Elise felt up to it.

She and Tom had just experienced the beauty and rich culture of Buenos Aires for a few days before arriving here at the estancia. Elise had loved the passion of the tango dancing shows in Buenos Aires, and the fact that you could even randomly find tango dancers performing at outdoor craft markets.

The food was delicious, and the city lived up to its reputation as the Paris of South America, with stunning architecture and a cosmopolitan vibe.

As she surveyed the beautiful pool and cabanas at the estancia, Elise couldn't remember a time when she had been so content. After such a crazy six months, finally everything fit together beautifully. Most importantly, she and Tom had been pretty much inseparable ever since the fateful day at Lawrence's cottage.

Tom and Miriam had come to terms on their divorce surprisingly quickly. And thanks to that lucrative settlement, plus Miriam's inheritance from her father's estate, Miriam should never have money worries. Police had cleared Miriam of any involvement in the plot against Tom, and she had recently moved back to North Carolina.

Miriam and Patrick were no longer together, and Patrick had relocated to Vancouver to become a sales executive at a gaming start-up.

Might as well put all that gambling experience to more productive use, Elise mused.

Tom had touched base with Lawrence that morning, and the Big Guy was busy as always, doing what he did best—making lots of money and sharing his insights with his fans—including new followers of his commentary on US cable TV. Elise and Tom spoke with Winston frequently, and he enjoyed his new role as Crystal Clere's regional VP for Canada. They would continue to work closely with Winston when she and Tom were established in California.

They hadn't been in touch with Liu because he was on special assignment with the RCMP's cybersecurity team, something that had Tom intrigued. Tom had told Elise he was hoping to hear more about it but realized that wasn't likely, as most of what Liu worked on would be classified.

As for Nate, there was no telling what would happen next. Hopefully, now that he had support from the trust fund, he wouldn't blow the opportunity to get back into his art and accomplish something positive. Only time would tell.

Tom had been sad to part from Titan, and Elise felt the same about leaving Cadette, but the horses would be well cared for until they moved back to Canada. Elise knew Cadette's owner would find a new rider soon to help keep the mare exercised, and Titan would have a trainer to keep him fit. Tom didn't want to bring Titan to California given the high forest fire risk around Santa Clara where they would be living.

Just then Elise looked up and saw Tom, tanned and relaxed, heading back toward her. He had gone to check their riding times for the next day, and Elise saw that he had picked up yerba mate for them to sip on.

When he sat down sideways facing Elise on the chaise next to her, he had a mischievous look on his face.

"What are you up to now?" Elise asked.

Tom set aside his drink and lowered himself onto one knee beside her, pulling out a small box. When he flipped it open, the light reflected off a stunning ring with a Columbian emerald surrounded by diamonds.

"Will you marry me, Elise Marie Armstrong?"

Elise smiled and said, "Yes, I will, Thomas John Oliver. And just in time too, because in about eight months there's going to be another Oliver in the world."

Tom looked dazed and reached for her hand.

Like concentric circles
From a pebble in a pond;
Someone's act of selfishness
Another's path gone wrong.

Webs of intricate design,
Patterns missed or meant;
Ebb and flow of circumstance
Integrity or intent.

—S. Grandy

Original acrylic painting by Roy Grandy: Collins Inlet on Georgian Bay

ACKNOWLEDGMENTS

"A good writer possesses not only his own spirit but also the spirit of his friends," Friedrich Nietzsche said. I hope that my family, friends, and even new contacts I met during the writing of this book will all recognize some of their spirit in *Devious Web*.

My first thank-you is to my husband, Roy Grandy, whose tolerance of hearing about "the book" and the chunks of time spent immersed in my computer has been much appreciated. His keen observations on everything from plotline to characters has made the creative process fun and the ultimate boost I needed to stay on track. Thanks for your caring support, Roy, and perhaps I'll consider a second novel where Detective Liu becomes the central character since you like him best.

To my daughter, Erin Bury, where do I even begin? Thanks for having served informally as my agent, reviewing the book at various stages of development and contributing in so many ways I can't list them all. You've saved me from using outdated terms like *portable computer*, *car phone*, *the net* instead of the *web*, and *attendants* instead of *bridesmaids*. I've enjoyed brainstorming with you about who will play all the characters in a movie someday, and we need to be there for Tom Oliver's casting calls! Everyone who knows you—especially me—is extremely lucky to have you in their life, Erin. Thank you for everything, and I love you lots!

To Meaghan Bury: You're an amazing editor and I so appreciated your review of the book and your encouragement. I know when your book is published it will be well received and I'm looking forward to that!

One of my earliest readers was my sister, Linda Hoover, a retired secondary school teacher and librarian. Her enthusiasm for the book meant so much because she reads constantly and because her academic background is in English and Latin. She could no doubt tell us what Latin roots *Pellucid* was derived from. Thank you, Linda, for always being in my corner, for your support throughout the writing process, and for being a final proofreader.

My sister, Sandra Chapman, has her hands full as a mom, grandmother, and great-grandmother to a burgeoning family, but she still found time to read the book along the way. Thanks for your encouragement, San, and for all the lovely things you do to stay connected with family.

There was no pressure for my brother, Dave Wilson, to read the book, given that—like my son-in-law, Kevin Oulds—he is an active guy who is more likely to wait for the movie than read a manuscript, which is totally fine. My sister-in-law, Maureen, was a valued early reader and has been a big supporter, and I thank her so much.

And now for my partner in crime—at least crimes devised against Tom—Stephanie Brett. Stephanie is a fun and insightful friend who poured creativity into discussions about the book and has been convinced of success from the get-go. Our fact-checking trip to Toronto to validate venue details was a real blast that I will never forget. Thank you, Steph, for sacrificing yourself to eat lobster spoons at ONE restaurant since I'm allergic! You proved those really are worthy of being described as the restaurant's signature dish! Your husband, Jeremy, previously a military pilot and now a commercial pilot, was a great help in advising on types of cars and planes to reference. Thank you both for all your support and encouragement.

Speaking of ONE, what a delight it was to meet general manager Tim Salmon and executive chef Darby Piquette, who were so kind to spend time with Stephanie and me, validating Tom and Lawrence's dining experience at ONE. And thanks also to DJ Rokhit, branch manager at TD Centre in downtown Toronto, who gave so generously of his time and expertise touring us through that historic bank and letting us explore the safe deposit vault (*safety* deposit vault in Canada) where purportedly Tom kept his valuable secrets. Sadly, we didn't come away with any cash souvenirs!

I was also lucky enough to connect with an ex–Toronto police officer who is now working on another police force and who is an avid reader. Thank you, Chris Ramsay, for taking the time to read the book and for your detailed and valuable input on the police-related aspects of the story.

Jeanne Ridgley, my friend and a retired nurse with lots of experience treating medical trauma, provided input related to Tom's injuries. I also want to credit my doctor, Dr. Vikie Bédard, who reviewed the final medical content and made my day by wanting to read more! Thank you, Jeanne and Dr. Bédard.

Janet Gosse, a friend and very early reader of *Devious Web*, inspired me to provide richer context for various scenarios in the book. I've also appreciated her husband Rick's ongoing support and his early read of the manuscript, so thanks to you both.

A shoutout goes to friends Diane Dorland Wright, Zbyszek (Zeb) Roter, and Michelle O'Brodovich who read early drafts of the manuscript and provided their perspective and encouragement.

Recent and much appreciated advance readers have included Thom Hill of North Carolina who was my former boss and mentor at Nortel, and Christine Ellison, a close friend and accomplished Human Resources leader in the finance sector.

A sincere shout-out goes to my publicist, Kathleen Schmidt, who is an insightful and supportive advisor. Thanks for your work publicizing *Devious Web*, and for sharing your wisdom in your amazing blog *Publishing Confidential* (https://kathleenschmidt.substack.com/).

I also want to recognize Kelley Keehn https://kelleykeehn. com, best-selling author of 11 books and a personal finance expert, who found time to provide a review for my novel and provide encouragement, which was so appreciated.

Much appreciation goes to SparkPress for selecting my manuscript and providing the platform for publishing *Devious Web*.

I also want to thank owner and manager Tina Spooner at Game Hill Stables where my horses, Chancey and Briosa, are boarded, for the great care and peace of mind that enabled me to have focused writing days without worrying about their well-being. We have been so lucky to be part of the Game Hill horse community of friends and fellow boarders.

Writing *Devious Web* has been a fun journey and learning experience, chronicled on my author website https:// shelleygrandy.com. Most importantly, I hope that you—my valued readers—enjoyed the book!

ABOUT THE AUTHOR

Shelley Grandy is a Canadian communications professional whose type-A personality and honors journalism degree from Ottawa's Carleton University fueled a career that started in newspapers and progressed to twenty-five years at high-tech company Nortel. She subsequently founded Grandy Public Relations Inc. and has supported tech sector clients in Ontario and Quebec for the past sixteen years. After writing countless press releases and technical articles for trade media, *Devious Web* is Shelley's debut fiction novel.

When not writing, Shelley enjoys intriguing Netflix-style productions and is known to frequently reference scenes from *Grace and Frankie*. You can also find her at the boarding stable with her horses, Chancey and Briosa. Shelley lives in Trenton, Ontario, Canada, with husband of thirty-plus years Roy, husky dog Luka, and cat Otto, within spoiling distance of her beautiful granddaughters, Emilia and Olivia Oulds.

Author photo © Tara McMullen Photography

Looking for your next great read?

We can help!

Visit www.gosparkpress.com/next-read
or scan the QR code below for a list
of our recommended titles.

SparkPress is an independent boutique publisher
delivering high-quality, entertaining, and engaging
content that enhances readers' lives, with a special
focus on commercial and genre fiction.